Pout, the chimera, half-man, half-ape, was in-corporated into one of the plants or vice versa. He was jammed in a squatting position, while the stems, entering at his buttocks, merged with his legs, his arms and his torso, emerging at knees, elbows, and through his abdomen and thorax. A large, yellow-petalled flower seemed to frame his face.

It was his face that rivetted Ikematsu's attention, while the chimera squirmed in dumb distress, glaring with huge piteous eyes. For in that face, set into it as if set in pudding, was the zen gun. The gun was his face, or a part of it. The barrel pointed straight out in place of a nose . . . the stock merged with and disappeared into Pout's pendulous mouth.

Ikematsu leaned toward the chimera. "How you loved your toy! Now it is truly yours!"

THE
ZEN
GUN

Barrington J. Bayley

DAW BOOKS, INC.
DONALD A. WOLLHEIM, PUBLISHER

1633 Broadway, New York, NY 10019

FIRST PRINTING, AUGUST 1983

1 2 3 4 5 6 7 8 9

DAW℠ ♖
BOOKS

DAW TRADEMARK REGISTERED
U.S. PAT. OFF. MARCA
REGISTRADA. HECHO EN U.S.A.

PRINTED IN U.S.A.

CHAPTER ONE

Around the blue, green and white planet, Ten-Fleet disposed itself with a suddenness that was intentionally frightening. On the diagrammatisation screens in the control centres of both sides, the criss-cross orbits of the hundred and forty ships resembled the electrons of a heavy atom orbiting an engorged nucleus like an enclosing web. In the first seconds of the occupation the planet's own service satellites, a gnat's haze, had been vapourised, the staffs of a dozen manned stations taken prisoner. Robbed of communications, the planet was helpless and nearly blind.

Meantime Ten-Fleet substituted its own satellite haze. Everything on and below the surface was being monitored at a resolution level of one to one.

Relaxing in his den, Admiral Archier could imagine the consternation now reigning on the planet. Its government would be ignorant—or so he hoped—of what he as a military man understood all too well, namely that to be in a position to blast a planet by missile, beam or blanket was merely an exercise in military impotence. The criterion of practical power was the capability to land effectives, and just as important, to take them off again.

Ten-Fleet was depleted. If it came to it, Archier would not properly be able to administrate the cowering population. Its dreadful weaponry was, in that sense, a threat that could be bluffed.

It was advisable, therefore, to conduct his business quickly, before the government down below began to draw conclusions from the fleet's inaction. The Admiral did not relish having to make a decision as to whether to punish the planet for recalcitrance.

Archier reclined on a mossy bank in the shade of an apple tree. Animals played and gambolled a short distance away: a dwarf elephant two feet tall; a dwarf giraffe whose head could

5

crane almost to Archier's shoulder; a chimp, and a bush baby almost as large.

Disengaging itself, the elephant strolled over. "The ruling council is in debate right now," it announced in a slightly trumpety voice. "According to bounce-back satellite reports, they are talking over ways to cheat us."

Archier smiled. "No doubt they think they can pass off decorticated murderers as artistic geniuses. Well, we've seen all that before."

The giraffe ambled over to rub its neck against his sleeve. "I hope they give us a good composer," he said in his soft, mild voice. "Would we be allowed to commission him before we make delivery to Diadem?"

"While we are in semi-autonomous status, yes."

"Admiral, they are asking to talk to us," the elephant chimed in.

Archier nodded. He patted the large grey head of his elephant adjutant, whose brain implant kept it in touch with all of Ten-Fleet's communications. "Come with me then, Arctus. I might need you to keep me informed."

From his present vantage point the mossy wood had no visible limits. But when Archier stepped behind the apple tree to stroll through the dappled light of the grove, Arctus padding along behind him, he was suddenly in a wide, carpeted corridor bearing a steady traffic of men, women, children and animals. A short walk brought him to the official audience chamber. A spider monkey looked up and lifted a hand in salute. Then it began to set up the meeting.

Admiral Archier took his cloak of rank from a nearby peg and self-consciously seated himself upon the throne before the view area. Subdued lights came on. He felt the mantle of imperial numinousness descend upon him. To those whose images now sprang to life in the view area his clean, pale features would seem majestic and almost angelically authoritative, and the glint in his eye would betoken a chilling perceptiveness.

He was looking into a council chamber. About twenty people sat around an oval table; there were no animals present. At the head of the table, raised a little above the others, was the Chairman of the Rostian Council, an elderly man who bore his years well, and who wore a white gown that made him look almost clinical. A short and neatly trimmed white beard sprouted from his chin.

The Chairman was the only one able to look directly at Archier without having to turn his head. The expression on his face was that of one who knew the weakness of his position and was forcing himself to bite back heartfelt defiance.

"Do I address the representative of the Imperial Directors?" he asked in a dry, acid tone.

"You do, but more specifically the Imperial Collector of Taxes," Archier answered lightly. "As already stated, you are twenty standard years in default. The matter is serious; your account must be settled forthwith."

"We are not wilfully in default," the Chairman said with steely grimness. "Ten years ago we offered to render all due services in credit, manufactured goods or rare materials. We received no reply."

"I am your reply. Your offer should not have been made. It bodes the Empire no service and is interpreted as attempted evasion of payment." Archier reached out his hand; the spider monkey placed a file of papers on it. "However, to clear the matter up, the Imperial Inspector of Revenues has agreed to reduce arrears by fifty percent—on condition that all future levies are paid promptly at the stipulated ten-standard-year intervals, delivery being your responsibility."

The Admiral bent his head to the papers before him. "These are the levies which will now be paid by you before we depart."

He began to read from a list. "One thousand two hundred and fifty-eight artists of the musical variety, comprising both composers and performers.

"One thousand two hundred and fifty-eight artists of the visual, tactile and odoriferous varieties.

"One thousand two hundred and fifty-eight practitioners of the literary and dramatic arts.

"Two thousand and twenty scientists of assorted disciplines.

"You are reminded that all persons must be human, not animal or construct, containing not more than two percent of dominant animal genes. All persons must reach at least Grade Twenty on the Carrimer Creativity Test that will be applied by Fleet psychologists. Further, at least one hundred persons should be of genius standard, or Grade Twenty-Five on the Carrimer Test."

Archier looked up and handed back the file to the spider monkey. The faces staring at him could only be described as stony.

Oh, I know what you're thinking. We would rather secede from the Empire, that's what you're thinking. But you dare not speak of rebellion, not openly, not even here on the fringe, while Ten-Fleet sweeps over your heads.''

"This traffic in people goes quite against the social philosophy we have evolved here on Rostia!" the Chairman protested. "It is slavery!"

"Do not despair, the cream of your nation will be exporting that philosophy into the Empire generally," Archier retorted amiably. "Your reluctance is a sad state of affairs. There was a time when the gifted among us competed for a chance to migrate to the heart of the Empire."

"Were that so, this tribute would hardly be necessary."

Archier leaned forward. "You have told me what you do not like. There is something *I* do not like. I do not like the word 'tribute.' I am here as a tax-gatherer. We all live under the law. Make arrangements for payment."

The Chairman bit his lip. "We shall need time if we are to do this. You come upon us suddenly."

"We shall not brook any delay. We shall know if you stall for time or plot any trickery against us. Therefore, I call on you to reassert your allegiance to the Empire." At this moment Archier became aware that Arctus the elephant was tugging at his sleeve with its trunk. He leaned aside. "What is it, Arctus?" he muttered.

The tiny elephant opened its maw and whispered hoarsely in Archier's ear. "A message from High Command!"

Straightening, Archier turned back to the Rostian Council. "Will you kindly begin your despatches within one rotation. Goodbye for now."

With that end to the conversation, hurried as it was, he rose, thanked the spider monkey, and left the audience room with Arctus. They passed through curtains of draped light: mauve, lavender, lilac, finally effervescent lemon.

Suddenly they were in the space-torsion room.

A nine-year-old boy was on duty, a son of one of the crew who had been given the job much as he might have been given a toy. With an eager sense of ceremony he presented Archier with the message, which had come in word form.

It was a directive, engraved in glowing letters on a sheet of yellow parchment. Archier murmured his thanks and scanned it.

After the addressing and classification codes came a terse instruction.

ESCORIA SECTOR IN CONDITION REBELLION. PROCEED IN FULL MAJESTY, OBJECT SUPPRESSION, CONDITION AUTONOMY. ENABLING DATA WILL FOLLOW.

Admiral Archier gazed at the parchment for some time, allowing the key phrases to sink in. *Full Majesty*. That meant he was to recognise no constraint on the deployment of the fleet's resources. *Condition Autonomy*. That meant that the fleet had the legal standing of a sovereign state. In theory it implied that the High Command had lost its power to act or had even collapsed. He, Archier, could behave as though *he* were the government of the Empire, responsible to no one.

If the rebellion in Escoria could not be dealt with, he could choose to obliterate all human life there—and was probably expected to do so. Instead of punishing the planet below by destroying a city or two, he could, likewise, annihilate it.

The disintegration of the Empire as an organised and effective entity was plainly proceeding apace.

He passed the parchment to Arctus. The elephant took the bottom edge in the tip of its trunk and raised the sheet before its face.

"Ah. This is promotion of sorts, sir."

"Is it?" Archier sounded doleful. "It bodes a less happy set of circumstances to me."

Ruefully he thought of the tax reprieve which now had inadvertently befallen Rostia. The dignity of the Empire would best be served, he thought, if Ten-Fleet were to leave without warning, as abruptly as it had come.

"Come, Arctus," he sighed, "let's to the Command Room."

Minutes passed. And then the web of orbits surrounding Rostia faded from the diagrammatisation screens, though the thousand or so satellites were expendable and remained, a replacement gift for the planet that, Admiral Archier feared, had slipped for the time being from the Empire's grasp.

As the fleet withdrew it was simultaneously reassembling itself into interstellar flight formation, gathering itself together like a school of fish, while each ship geared up its feetol drive. The path of exit from Rostia's solar system was nearly parallel to the orbital plane, and as the fleet passed close to the primary gas giant a cursory message reached Archier from the environs scan officer.

"Methorian ship descending towards gas giant, sir."

Archier accepted an imaging fix. He saw the alien vessel, a great bulky pod caught within a baroque-looking cradle, and watched as it slipped into the swirling clouds of the huge planet.

"I'm hazy on recognition, Arctus. What is it?"

"It's a Methorian cargo carrier," Arctus informed him.

"Oh," Archier murmured, incurious as to whether the alien settlement was merely an outpost or even a fully developed planetary society. As with several other alien interstellar empires, the Methorian empire interpenetrated the human one but had practically no contact with it. Given the scale of interstellar distances, and the variety of worlds, there could be little concept of exclusive territory as between oxygen-breathing humans, hydrogen-breathing methanogens, salines, high-temperature acidophiles, and so forth, all inhabiting types of planet of no value to the others.

So the Methorian presence in a system from which the Empire was, for the time being, forced to retreat, signified nothing. The gas giant flipped from the screen, and at the same time from Archier's notice. In its place he saw the local star field, almost a cluster in its own right, lighting up lacy gas trails to one side of it.

Are we to give this up? he thought. *No! It's ours. It must remain ours.* The Empire claimed each one of these stars as its own property. That aliens might hold a similar view was of no consequence, any more than the owner of a stretch of forest would bother himself with the territorial struggles of the animals living in it. Vast dramas might be unfolding in any of these alien empires, without human society being in the least aware of it.

There was a flurry on the screen as the metric fields generated by the feetol drives of a hundred and forty ships intermeshed to form a single field enclosing the fleet like a bubble. By then they were already travelling faster than light; now their velocity increased a hundredfold.

Ten-Fleet was *en route* to Escoria Sector.

Evening, fleet time, and Admiral Archier left his quarters to go strolling through his flagship *ICS Standard Bearer*.

ICS prefixed the names of all Star Force vessels. It stood

for *Imperial Council Ship*, the Imperial Council having replaced the Imperial Directorate—a cybernetic decision-making system—nearly a century ago. The short-lived Directorate, a product of the Anti-archist Revolution, had in its turn replaced the Imperial Civil Service, which had been commanded by an hereditary line of genetically optimised Emperor Protectors.

Though Archier would readily admit that the overthrow of the principle of personal overlordship was praiseworthy on ideological grounds, its practical results had been far from beneficial. The Directorate had so completely failed to handle the affairs of the Empire that an official doctrine of machine unsentience had ensued. Ironically, that doctrine was now crippling the Empire's industrial capacity because of the disaffection of the robot workforce. The collective leadership of the Council was doing its best to arrest the Empire's progressive decay and disintegration, but it too was failing. Archier, in common with many officers under his command, privately believed—though it was politically unwise to say so too openly—that the disinheriting of the Protector had been a tragic mistake.

Haunting music, exotic scents, drifted through the salons and dance halls of the flagship, which like all major war vessels of Imperial Star Force was one huge pleasure ship. It could hardly have been otherwise; the vessel had been built in the Imperial yards and its crew all belonged to that part of the Empire's starclouded heartland known as Galactic Diadem. To such people, sybaritic luxury was as natural and necessary as the air they breathed.

The talented artists and scientists collected as taxes by Ten-Fleet—it had become its chief function—were often open-mouthed with astonishment when brought aboard. Archier had heard them apply the word "decadent" more than once. For his part, the outlying worlds from which the taxes were levied seemed rude and barbarous. He viewed their unreliability with disdain, all the more so because their contribution was so vital if the Empire was to survive.

"Good evening, Admiral."

"Good evening, Madam." Archier's response was cordial to the handsome matron who lounged against the frame of an arcaded entrance. Beyond it, in a kind of gymnasium, a group of ten-year-old girls in leotards were learning a dance routine. They were nymphs—junior members of Priapus' People, one of Diadem's finest dance and sex troupes, for which training began at the age of eight. Already these girls would be experts in a variety of erotic arts, coached in the giving of sexual pleasure.

An entertainment by their more mature colleagues was scheduled for later. Barely glancing at the lissom, lunging bodies, Archier walked on, to enter the main salon. There, airy melodies blared softly over a hum of conversation. He tried to forget his anxieties, to let himself relax.

A satin-sheathed young figure turned as he passed.

"Dance with me, Admiral."

The face that smiled wistfully at him was senile, artificially aged to that of a ninety-year-old's, though the girl was in fact about twenty. Her cheeks and jowls were wrinkled and sagging, caked with cosmetic, her green eyes spiteful and rheumy. The combination of an ancient face and a young body was to be seen throughout the salon; it was the current fashion in feminine beauty, a concept that changed rapidly in all sophisticated societies. It said much for the strength of social conditioning that the sight of the sexually trained girl children had aroused Archier hardly at all, but when the withered, decayed cheek of his dance partner was placed against his, a thrill went right through him.

He considered asking her to his table, even though he knew the current fad in her age group was to refuse all sexual liaisons. She had been made pure virgin, her hymen surgically restored, all memory of past sexual encounters expunged from her mind. However, when the tune ended and they ceased to dance a wheezing voice accosted him from behind.

"Ah, there you are, Admiral!"

A pig whom he recognised as Acting Fire Command Officer of Fleet Weapons Division had come bustling into the salon. A trifle wearily, he acknowledged the creature. By the regulations officers of command rank were supposed to be human, but human personnel were so scarce it had become the practice to give animals acting rank instead. Pigs appeared particularly suited to this role, and indeed eager for it.

Archier's Fire Command Officer seemed exasperated. He grunted, raising a bristled snout. "Not a very successful day, Admiral!"

Murmuring a polite goodbye to the old-faced young woman, Archier sauntered with the animal towards the buffet. "The times we live in cause much confusion," he admitted ambiguously.

"Confusion? *I* suffer from no confusion!" The pig thrust his snout in a trough to root for tidbits, while Archier surveyed the delicacies laid out on the buffet tables. He picked up a tiny flask and sipped a cool, creamy, thick purple fluid from it through a straw. The cannabis-based drink made him feel better almost immediately.

The pig, on the other hand, seemed only to grow more agitated. He took his head out of the trough as though unable to contain himself any longer. "Admiral, I waited and waited for you to order a strike. And what happened? We simply left and did nothing!"

"We were ordered away," Archier said amiably. "There was no time to complete collection."

"Even so, we should have left them something to remember us by!" spluttered the pig. "Vapourise a city or two. Beam a disintegration trail across the main continent. These worlds need to be shown who's master!"

Thoughtfully Archier sucked up the rest of the purple drink. "It wouldn't really have been fair. They hadn't actually refused payment yet. It wasn't their fault we had to leave."

"It *was* their fault we were there at all! By the Simplex, Admiral, what's going to happen to the Empire if all we're going to be is *fair*? Firmness is what's needed!" The pig shook his head and let out a long, troubled snuffling sound. "Sometimes I despair of you humans!"

He waddled away. A voice spoke near Archier. "I wonder if the appointment was wise in that pig's case. I've noticed he gets upset when he doesn't get a chance to play with the fleet's firepower."

With a shrug Archier acknowledged a young man in the sheened dress uniform of the Drop Commando. "People naturally like to do their job—animals more so than humans, if you ask me. Anyway, a post like that calls for keenness. It needs a pig, or feline."

The commando nodded. "My cheetahs and dogs strain at the leash every time we invest a planet. It's difficult explaining why we can't go, sometimes."

"What we really need are more humans."

"Don't we all know that!" The commando laughed and

helped himself to a leaf-dish of crunchy diced vegetables. "At least, in the Force we do. But try telling civilians."

Tossing the empty flask into a waste slot, Archier turned away. In his mind he saw Galactic Diadem, laid out like a map. Imperial worlds trailed out of the glowing starbank like ragged tentacles from some monster octopus, merging and dissipating into the fringe worlds—planets where Imperial control had become weak of late.

In theory the Empire claimed sovereignty over the whole galaxy, anticipating a time when mankind would be present throughout the galactic disk. In fact, if the galaxy were viewed from afar the extent of Imperial power would be seen as a fairly small though visible blotch, and whether that blotch would now be further extended was becoming, to many minds, problematical.

One, and perhaps the chief difficulty, was the drastically declining birth rate of Diadem and its close environs. The human population of Diadem, which could be thought of as ruling mankind much as one imperial country would once have ruled other countries (though it was never admitted that any such thing as political division existed) was about one million. To that could be added a few tens of millions of animals with artificial intelligence who assisted in the administration of the Empire, and of course some hundreds of millions of robots who were vital economically but were denied citizenship.

But neither animals nor robots were artistically or scientifically creative, and one million people, spread over such a vast region, offered too small a reservoir of creative talent to encourage confidence in the future. What was more, the situation was getting worse. The next generation would see an Empire manned by only seven hundred thousand. Eventually the population might stabilise, but Diadem would lose the mental strength necessary for its self-appointed destiny.

The remedy was typical of the Empire's methods: a levy of artists, scientists and philosophers drawn from the fringe and vassal worlds which mainly had their own governments and whose total population could be measured in the hundreds of millions. Whether the personnel tax was succeeding in its aims was debatable. Some of the dragooned artists and scientists certainly found their carefree lives in Diadem to their liking and stayed—particularly those from social regimes which, while more vigorous, were also more restrictive. But the total liberty inalienable to full Imperial citizens in Diadem—and that included anyone with 90 percent or more human genes—virtually made it impossible to prevent anyone from clandestinely leaving, should they be so inclined. Not even the threat to punish the home worlds of defectors had always proved effective.

And so Diadem provided a narrowing base of human resource from which to rule the galaxy. Neither was the task taken on by those few determined to maintain the Empire made any easier by the disinterest shown by the majority of humans in Diadem. Hence the preponderance of youth to be found among the crews of Star Force.

Yet it said much for the Empire's self-confidence that Diadem's one million inhabited nearly a thousand planets, and still managed to hold sway over a yet higher number whose populations were much larger. True, the Empire's integrity outside Diadem was sustained only by permanent deployment of the star fleets (in their heyday there had been thirty-six of them; now there were only five) whose role it was to suppress rebellion, collect taxes from defaulters—and, most important, try to prevent secessionist-minded worlds from acquiring star fleets of their own.

The commando officer trailed after Archier. It was as if he shared his thoughts, for he touched his elbow and said, "I hope you don't mind my asking, Admiral, but I've been meaning to ask you how old you are."

Archier paused. His eye had caught the coloured *incoming* lights glowing over the intermat kiosks at the far end of the salon. Guests were arriving from other ships in Ten-Fleet, making use of the matter transmission facility the fleet was able to use while in fast feetol formation. Gorgeous finery, ostentatious dress uniforms (officers of third rank and over were permitted to design their own) burgeoned from the kiosks as the visitors stepped forth.

"That's all right," Archier said. "I shall be twenty-one on my next birthday. And I've been Admiral of Ten-Fleet for more than three years."

CHAPTER TWO

Pout's cage had no visible bars. Bars might have been an improvement. Then at least he would have been able to see the limits of his prison.

To the casual eye he lived in a bare but pleasant room, at liberty to leave by either of two doors or to approach the people or robots who occasionally passed through. In reality he was confined to one small corner of this room. In the floor there was a hole for his wastes. A slot in the wall flapped open at intervals and delivered edible monotonous substances. A faucet squirted water in measured amounts whenever he pressed a lever. Sometimes he would play with the water, watching it swirl round the concavity in the floor and disappear down the waste hole.

And there *were* bars: invisible ghost bars of pain—jagged, flashing pain that sent him mewling and cringing into the join of the walls if he tried to leave his corner. He knew that they were actual bars, because there were gaps in between them. In the past, by trial and error, he had managed to find a gap and put his arm through almost to the shoulder.

Pout could see that other people weren't constrained in this way. Other people didn't look like him, either. They didn't have his big cup-shaped ears, or his simian-like features (with the elongated lips that, though he wasn't aware of it, had given him his name), or his over-long arms. Also, they had many satisfactions that were denied him. They smiled and looked pleased often. On this score Pout's imagination was a dim, smouldering ember. His response to anything outside his experience was hatred and resentment, but he was not introspective enough to know that these feelings drew their heat from envy.

There was one person more familiar to him than any other, and this was Torth Nascimento, curator of the museum where Pout lived. One day, as Pout was squatting over the excre-

ment hole, Nascimento entered in the company of a stranger.
The latter, a tall man with straw-coloured hair and mild blue
eyes, paused. He inspected the scene without the least concern for Pout's privacy.

"Is this another of your chimeras, Torth?"

"Yes," Nascimento drawled. "That's Pout."

"He's an odd-looking customer," the newcomer remarked
as Pout finished his business. "What's he made of?"

"Just about every primate there is. Mostly, though, he's
gibbon, baboon and human."

"Can he talk?"

"Oh yes. Intellectually he's very nearly human. Unfortu-
nately his morals are execrable . . . so much so that we have
to keep him locked up." He pointed to a light in the ceiling.
It was a warning that a pain projector was in operation. "The
robot file clerks took care of him in his infancy. They even
taught him how to look into the files, so in a queer sort of
way he's had an education."

"Your file clerks? Are they the *only* company he's ever
had?"

"Oh come, Lopo, don't be so disapproving," Nascimento
said, glancing at the expression on his guest's face. "There's
nothing actually *illegal* in making chimeras."

"Not if you have a licence for it."

"I'm sure I'd get one if the question came up. This *is* a
museum, remember." Nascimento paused thoughtfully. "You
know, I'm not surprised the chimeric approach was abandoned in Diadem. Inter-species gene manipulation isn't as
simple as it sounds. So *difficult* to hit on a good mix . . . just
look at Pout here if you want a case in point. Compounded
entirely of the primate family, the best nature has to offer, yet
a perfectly horrid creature. Now you've brought my attention
to him I must remember to have him destroyed. He's not even
interesting enough to be an exhibit.

The other man bristled. "What's this I hear? You propose
to destroy a bona-fide second-class citizen of the Empire?"

"Is he? Yes, I suppose he is. All right, don't get excited."
Nascimento ushered him out of the room—really an enlarged
section of passageway—where Pout lived. The two were
silent until they reached Nascimento's office, where the curator shooed away a couple of robots who were playing chess.

Lopo de Cogo sat down. Nascimento set a tiny glass of
purple liqueur before him. "I don't know why you object to

my making chimeras, Lopo. I thought you sympathised with
the Whole-Earth-Biota party?''

"Please, Torth, that was in our student days,'' Lopo said
uneasily. "All right, we'll forget about chimeras. I'm afraid
I've something more serious to talk about. Is it true you've
been giving artificial intelligence to non-mammals? That *is*
illegal, whichever way you look at it.''

"I'm not sure I agree. You seem to be forgetting my
museum has a special charter covering all the sciences.''

De Cogo bit his lip. If taxed about his behaviour Nascimento
invariably referred to some ancient warrant granted by a ruler
of the planet in days past and never revoked. He never,
however, had been able to produce this warrant.

Hitherto de Cogo's old friendship with the eccentric curator
had overriden both his duty as an official inspector and his
personal feelings. But it was becoming plain to him that
Nascimento's ethics (and perhaps his mind) had reached a
point of non-recovery.

Also, the fellow was clearly a bungler. His remarks on the
difficulty of gene-mixing were the cry of an amateur barely
literate in the field. In Diadem chimerics was an advanced
art. Chimeras had outnumbered pure humans there in the
Empire's heyday. Cell fusion had begun to replace sex as a
method of reproduction.

That had been the Whole-Earth-Biota concept: that the
dividing lines between species would disappear and the entire
mammalian class of old Earth would merge into a single
society. But the Biotist philosophy, as it was called, had
foundered. It alarmed many pure humans to see the genes of
Homo sapiens melting away into a common pool, and radical
gene mixing eventually became unfashionable. It was mainly
used now for cosmetic purposes. People in Diadem would
take their zygotes to a chimericists to give an unborn child a
trace of some particular animal. A touch of tiger, for instance,
added a personal magnetism that was instantly recognisable.

Although Diadem was overwhelmingly populated by animals,
de Cogo doubted if the Biotists would ever be able seriously
to revive their cause. There were too many advantages in
giving animals artificial intelligence instead, altering their
genes only to adjust them for size, or occasionally in place of
surgery, to give them speech organs. Humans remained the
master race. Animal intelligence, previously unpredictable,
no longer depended on a successful gene mix—even humans

were given adplants sometimes to bring their intelligence up to scratch.

On one thing, however, both the old Biotists and the modern Diademians were agreed. Neither human genes nor artificial intelligence should be conferred upon non-mammals. "Whole-Earth-Biota" was really a euphemism for "Whole-Earth-Mammalia."

De Cogo had to press the point. "Please give me a direct answer, Torth."

Nascimento shrugged.

"Please, you must tell me, Torth. You know how the law regards this. A mammal has emotional sensitivity—it can be civilised. But an intelligent reptile, or raptor—it has no feelings! It's forever a savage and a danger to others!" Officially such creatures could never be regarded as sentient, no matter what their intellectual capacity.

Nascimento giggled. "I've got to admit an intelligent snake remains a most uncivil sort of being, not really a person at all. But when you run a museum you feel the need to be *comprehensive*—you follow me?"

"So it's true," de Cogo sighed.

Smiling, Nascimento began to reminisce. "Adplanting is so simple it can even be applied to primitive orders, like arthropods. I might as well admit—I've amused myself with that as well. Boris was my favourite. A wolf spider."

"Intelligence at the service of a *spider?*" De Cogo was bewildered. "But what's the point of that? A spider doesn't have a real mind—it's just a behavioural machine!"

"Well, I was bored. That's why I gave him the genes to be big—he was the size of a pony. Except that an arthropod that large can't even stand up unmodified, so, surgical engineering—a prosthetic internal skeleton! I wish I could show him to you, but I'm afraid to say there was a mishap and he escaped. He had the craftiness to scamper well away from here, of course, the rascal. I hear he became the terror of the Kolar district before he was eventually destroyed!" Nascimento gave a high-pitched laugh.

"You're mad," de Cogo whispered to himself. He cleared his throat. "Torth, you know I'm here in an official capacity. I've tried to tell you before that you're going too far. This time—"

"This is an ancient institution," Nascimento interrupted,

"and petty laws are passing affairs. We're not bound by them here. We have a longer perspective."

"*Everyone* is bound by them, Torth." De Cogo stopped, aware he did not have the other's attention. Torth was bending over the chess board vacated by the robots, smiling at the unfinished game. Then his fingers moved to the keys and switched a few pieces round.

"Poor Crinklebend never wins," he explained. "Just thought I'd give him a leg-up. Now, what were we saying? Ah yes, rules and regulations. My dear old friend, how can you be serious? This isn't Diadem, it's Escoria Sector. Imperial edicts aren't much more than hopeful advice here. Besides—" Nascimento poked a finger at the ceiling—"according to what I hear there's a rebellion brewing up there. The Empire looks likely to be pushed right out."

"Even if that does happen, do you imagine the rebels are going to let the region descend into lawlessness?"

"Oh, they aren't Biotists, are they?" Torth asked anxiously.

"No, I don't think so."

"Good. Anyway, no one's going to take any interest in us. It's a funny thing, you know, how the meaning of the word 'Earth' has changed. It's used today in a biological sense— 'whole-Earth-biota.' But actually it refers to a planet. *This* planet, Lopo. This is *Earth*, remember?"

"Yes," said de Cogo vaguely. It scarcely occurred to him to make the association. It was as if "Earth" was two different words that sounded the same. "What has that got to do with anything?"

"Everything," Nascimento told him airily. "This is the forgotten original world, a total backwater. Nobody ever comes here, so what makes you think the rebels will, even if they do win? And as the governing council you claim to represent is almost as impotent as Diadem herself, what I'm saying is I can do anything I like, really. So stop moaning at me, Lopo!"

With those words Nascimento rose to his feet, and adopting the manner of one who has disposed of a troublesome importuner, sauntered from the room.

The curator's words of that afternoon had struck terror into Pout. It comforted him not at all that the visitor had tried to come to his aid: Pout knew that Nascimento would not be stopped by anyone else's opinion. His only hope of survival appeared to be for the curator to forget his decision.

He felt extra terror, but also surprise, therefore, when de Cogo once again appeared before him that evening. The inspector looked him over, compassion in his pale blue eyes.

"Poor half-monkey," he murmured. "No mother, no father—what a substitute Torth has made! Try not to blame him—I think his reason went a long time ago. Well, at least I can do something to alleviate *your* suffering."

Stepping to the wall, he slid back a panel Pout had never known existed. In the ceiling the signal light went out.

"Come. Your bars are gone."

Pout cringed. He could not believe what this man seemed to be offering him; it was a trick. Looking at the woebegone creature, de Cogo was suddenly reminded of another experiment of Nascimento's, the birdman. Lacking voice, unable to articulate language in either spoken or written form, this unfortunate knew only one mode of expression: the C melody saxophone. He played it like an angel whenever he wanted to communicate, uttering tunes and brilliant cascades of notes instead of sentences, trills and arpeggios instead of words. Nascimento had claimed this was a sophisticated form of birdsong, and that the musician was a man-blackbird he had (illegally but unrepentantly) fused. Suspicious at the lack of any physical chimeric signs (though the birdman was rather gawky), de Cogo had discovered the truth. The "birdman" was a pure human Nascimento had raised from birth, using accelerative growth hormones. The reason why he was speechless was that he had been systematically denied any opportunity to learn language. Music, in which he received intensive training, had been his only permitted form of communication. Nascimento had even resorted to putting the growing child in deep freeze between music lessons, to guard against nonmelodic imprinting. He regarded the experiment as a resounding success: the speech centre, a left hemisphere brain function, became untrainable. The left hemisphere, the site of intuitive abilities including music, emerged as the only channel for meaning.

Indignant at seeing a first-class citizen imprisoned, de Cogo had obtained his freedom. Presumably he still wandered the Earth somewhere, as a tormented minstrel, able to convey the most rarefied feelings but not a single fact.

But he doubted if he could persuade Nascimento, in his

present mood, to see reason in the case of Pout. He beckoned.
"I am your friend. I will help you to freedom."

Pout recalled the way de Cogo had spoken for him earlier.
Cautiously, hopefully, he allowed himself to be wheedled
from the corner. He passed through where the invisible bars
had been. There was no pain.

He was standing on a different part of the floor!

His blood raced. It had been so long!

"Put this on," de Cogo told him gently, holding out a
yellow garment with a bib-like front attached to short trousers.
Pout pawed at it. Eventually, at de Cogo's instructions, he
managed to fasten it on him. Then he stood awkwardly,
shoulders bowed, swivelling his eyes from side to side, wondering what to do. He would have liked to be able to hurt his
rescuer, to injure him or even to kill him somehow, but he
was not physically strong and he was afraid to attack him.

"Follow me," said de Cogo crisply. Pout shuffled after the
inspector; who led him through a long corridor, and then
through a low-roofed gallery he vaguely remembered.

Then he turned left and they emerged onto a timber veranda.
A warm breeze blew on Pout. Ahead of him, savannah-like
grassland stretched to the horizon. The sun was mellow,
hanging over the scene like a burnished lamp.

Though he was unreceptive to the beauty of the landscape,
it stirred something in him: a yearning common to creatures,
whether base or noble.

Freedom! Freedom to live! To enjoy!

De Cogo, even while edging away slightly from the rank-
smelling creature beside him, sensed this yearning. "You
must make your own way now," he muttered quickly, "for I
have done all I can. You are at liberty, as a second-class
citizen of the Empire, if you know what that means."

He paused. "The galaxy is wide, but hazardous, of course.
You must make of life what you will. I wish you luck—now
go, before the curator discovers what I have done."

Pout stared blankly, until given a shove towards the steps
leading to the ground. He stumbled down them, nearly falling,
wondering if this was some trick.

When his bare feet touched the ground, the sensation was
like nothing he had known before. The grass tickled, and
unable to restrain himself, he flung himself down in it and
rolled from side to side.

When he paused from this luxury to look up, the man was gone.

If he lay down, the grass seemed to cover him. Pout began to think. To get away from here quickly was good advice. And yet . . .

He felt frightened and helpless. What he needed was a weapon. A hand scangun he could hide in his new garment and use if he was threatened (or, he thought excitedly, on anyone he didn't like). Then he would feel less defenceless.

The pale green buildings of the museum stood scattered all around him. Pout, in a partial and confused way, was familiar with the layout. He had peeked into the data files when in the care of the robots, who had presumed that museum administration was the only thing anyone could be interested in. That hangar-like structure, with the grey metallic tinge, was the weapons house. He clearly remembered it was the weapons house.

The museum rarely had casual visitors, but in theory was supposed to be open to all comers. Nascimento had taken a precaution with the weapons house: its entrance was from the house of ancient-style footwear, a small and dusty gallery which gave the peruser no idea that the unprepossessing door led not to a cleaning closet but to a complete and treasured armoury . . .

Crawling through the grass, Pout made his way by degrees to where he felt he could run upright without being seen. Soon he had slipped through the vine-wreathed door of the ancient footwear house.

Stacked all around him were cases of shoes of every description—boots, clogs, slippers, in an endless but boring series, each pair carefully displayed and described. Pout did not glance at them. He satisfied himself he was alone, then slipped to the half-hidden door that led to a bare, square corridor, whose length he sprinted.

Then through the other door at the far end, an imposing and heavy door, needing all his strength to push it open.

Guns! Guns of every type!

In pride of place in the centre of the hangar was a huge feetol cannon such as were used by fighting starships. Pout experienced no curiosity as to how Nascimento could have acquired so impressive a weapon, for he did not know what it was apart from the fact that it was a very big gun, nor that it was impossible to make it work unless installed in a starship. He just stood, glorying in its sense of power.

Nervously he coughed. The sound echoed around the building, but for the moment he was not worried. Even the robots rarely came here. Usually the only time the heavy door opened was when a new exhibit was to be put on display.

He began to stroll past the cases, unsure as to how the exhibition was organised. He peered at weapon after weapon, but being unable to read could make no sense of descriptive plates. Finally he leaned against a case to stare at a long rifle with stock of mother-of-pearl and a golden barrel. Suddenly a soft voice spoke out of the air, startling him.

"Force rifle, thirty-first century. This weapon projects a radiant beam whose main effect is pressure. It will punch a hole in ten-point titanium at a range of . . ." Pout continued listening in fascination as the voice went on to detail specification and history of usage. Most of it, however, was incomprehensible to him, and the gun was bigger than he wanted.

He passed on. All the guns in the section were of the long sort, and they all seemed to be old. Where were the scanguns? Scanguns were really the only kind he had heard about. When with the robots, he had seen something on the data files. Though he didn't quite realize it, what he had seen was a fragment of an animated drama with psych-dimension—that is, it used a set of subliminal signals to manipulate the feelings of the watcher and make him feel a part of the action. In the fragment, there had been a shoot-out between people using scanguns. It was the most thrilling thing Pout had ever participated in. Because, of course, the watcher-identification was with the victor.

Rounding a corner, he came to a new section. Here the cases were smaller. Handguns!

But they seemed very old. He peered at the first one, and pressed against the side of the case to evoke the explanatory voice as he had just learned to do.

"Colt forty-five, nineteenth century. This weapon projects lead bullets at a velocity of . . ."

He heard no more than the first few words. Nineteenth century! What century was it now? He wasn't sure, but it was a lot more than the nineteenth.

Quickly he walked up the aisle past a long line of variegated handguns, hoping he would at last come to the modern scangun section. He could not, however, resist a look at some of the guns of the past, with their strange handgrips, their barrels that sometimes were fluted, sometimes snub-nosed, or square, or slitted—or no barrel at all—and their variously shaped triggers, studs and slides. In his ignorance it did not occur to Pout that in all probability not a single weapon in the collection would be complete with ammunition or charge, and many would not even be in working order. His idea of a gun was something he could simply pick up and shoot people with.

He thought he heard a sudden noise and stopped in fright. There was nothing. But then his eye lit on the case nearest to him, and he lingered to inspect its contents.

The gun was unprepossessing. Its handgrip and shaft seemed to be made mostly of wood or some grainy material. It was light in colour, as if the wood had been carved with a knife and then left untreated. Indeed, it could have been a toy.

The barrel, or shaft, was studded with buttons and was rectangular in shape. The stock was raked just a little, and lacked either sight or range-finder. Pout would have passed on, but some indefinable quality in the gun made him pause again. He pressed the side of the cabinet.

"*Electric gun, date unknown. Connection with Bushido. Has sympathetic circuits. Projects electricity.*"

That was all. None of the lengthy details on performance, construction and history that accompanied the other exhibits. For some reason this absence of information made Pout want to see the gun work. He searched for some means of switching off the screen separating him from the exhibit, and finding none, put his hand directly into the case.

He felt the pressure of the force-field resisting his hand. His fingers closed over the stock. As he had guessed, it was wood, a friendly-feeling substance. As he lifted it, this feeling seemed to transmit itself to him through his skin, and quiet words spoke in his mind.

"*I am yours.*"

But as soon as he had taken the gun from its case another quiet voice spoke, not in his mind but in the air. "*You have removed an exhibit from its case. Please replace the exhibit at once. An attendant has been summoned.*"

Pout whirled about, looking for the source of the voice, his mouth open with alarm.

Instinctively his forefinger pushed the long trigger-stud obtruding from the stock just beneath the shaft.

The result was unexpected. A row of short pale glowing lines, pink in colour, appeared in the air, stitching through space. The row had emanated from the end of the gun's shaft.

Looking afresh at his new acquisition, Pout grinned and felt pleased. Perhaps it wasn't a scangun (he couldn't see any control to make it scan) but it worked!

"*I note you have not yet replaced the exhibit,*" the soft voice said after a pause. "*Please do so, as the attendant is about to arrive.*" Pout's grin turned to a snarl, lips pulled back over the yellow teeth in his protruding jaw. He heard a near-silent purring behind him, and looked round to see a small robot wheeling towards him along the aisle.

Where had it come from? Pout hadn't heard the door open. Pout didn't know it, but this was no more than an idler robot, such as stood in a recess in every department of the museum and wheeled out only to deliver guided tours, lectures, or to caution visitors. It could not have done him any harm. But to Pout it represented the power of Torth Nascimento and he was terrified of it.

His whole body shook as he pointed his new gun in front of him and pressed the firing stud. He did not even train the muzzle on the target properly. The pale pink stitching appeared from the shaft, in a straight line to begin with, but then curving round until it terminated at the cranium of the little robot.

The robot did not explode or burn up or reduce itself to ash, as he had seen on the vid drama. It simply stopped.

The curved line of stitching stayed there, hanging in the air, until Pout took his finger off the firing stud. Then it vanished.

Standing half-crouched for a while, his heart pounding, Pout eventually crept up to the robot. It still did not move.

Then, with a shout of triumph, he knocked it right over. It clattered on its side, rolling from side to side until it became still.

He had killed it!

In his joy he turned and sprayed the weapons house with stitch fire. There was no visible effect; everything remained the same as it was. But the accusing voice did not bother him again, and he retreated to the doorway, tugged it open with an effort and ran down the passageway, through the house of ancient footwear and into the open.

Dusk was coming on. Pout began to contemplate the journey across the savannah, wondering if he would be cold at night and what might lie at the far end. He was almost loath, at the thought of it, to leave his warm, dreary corner.

His eyes scanned the museum complex. Now he was leaving, his hatred of Nascimento took on a poignant aspect. If only he could satisfy himself on that score first . . .

And why not? As the suggestion blossomed, like a blood-red rose, in his mind, a light popped on in a building some distance away. Through its window a figure was vaguely visible, moving to and fro and holding something in its hand.

Nascimento!

It was like being offered something delicious to eat. It seemed that his feet moved him without any prompting on his part, closer to the building where the light shone, and round to the side where he found a door.

There, his nerve failed him momentarily. He clutched the gun. Its grained stock comforted him; it felt *right*, sitting there in his hand. A quiet, murmuring voice in his head seemed to be saying, *"I am yours. You can maim and you can kill, with your zen gun."*

Zen? What was zen? The question died in Pout's mind as he pushed open the door, the gun pointed in front of him.

A screen made of coloured glasslike material stood on the other side of the door. It scarcely impeded the view of the scene in the room, however. Nascimento, his saturnine features amiable and relaxed, stood in the middle of the floor. In one hand he held a long-necked glass filled with a hazy green liquid. In the other, was a scangun.

Standing near the wall to the right of Pout were two people who were new to him. One was of medium height—a little shorter than Nascimento—and his black hair was swept clear of his pale, bony face and tied in a knot at the back of his head. There was a look of alert tension about him. His garb was strange: a loose white garment over which was fastened a sort of harness reaching from shoulder to knee, adorned at points by hooks and various fastenings.

Beside him stood a boy: blue-eyed, fair-haired, and with a faintly golden cast to his skin. His tunic and breeches had a flowery blue pattern, and he was unblinking as he stared at Nascimento.

The stranger in the harness spoke to the museum curator. "Your mendacity is of the sort that is total and shameless. In a way it is almost talented, for not everyone can win the trust of a warrior.''

"Not total," Nascimento replied evenly. "To enter the museum carrying weapons *is* forbidden; that much was true. I was surprised to see how trustingly you divested yourself of them. You see, *kosho,* it is your own respect for tradition that has betrayed you. I find that fitting. Like trapping a bee with sugar.''

"And the antique gun you promised to show me? That, I suppose, does not exist.''

"As a matter of fact—well, that's of no moment. What I need from you now is for you to adjust yourself to your new situation—which, being of a trained, flexible and serene mind I'm sure you can do. One word of warning, though," Nascimento added quickly as the man in harness made a stirring motion, "don't plan anything sudden. I have a sympathetic receiver trained on you both, connected to a high-power pulse blast. It will know if you intend a hostile move and will respond before ever you can make it.''

The other man smiled slightly, as though to inform Nascimento that he could deceive the sympathetic receiver. Nascimento slurped from his glass and waved his scangun. *"When a sage is about to act, he always appears slightly dull eh, kosho?* You see, I know a little about your discipline. As curator of this museum, I know a little about everything.''

"Very well, tell me why you have lured me here.''

"It is something you might well appreciate. You see, *kosho,* I feel a great duty towards this museum. It has existed for centuries. It was, of course, mostly destroyed during the action of eighty-three—what a barbarous episode!—but I have worked unstintingly to try to restore it and collect together the exhibits. I see the museum as a repository of everything that has been accomplished by this old planet—the original source of human civilisation. Below ground is a department the public is kept away from. There I have a collection of human types of special interest, particularly those that are associated with Earth. You have heard of the genetic statesmen? Purely altruistic, designed to give society the best possible leadership? Well, I have one! Raised from scratch, from the old codes. I also have a clone of Vargo Gridban, the man whose work eventually gave us the feetol drive, raised from the same record collection . . .

"But genetic codes will never, of course, give me a *kosho.*

They are the result of training. I have no *kosho*. They are too
hard to find, would not enter willingly into captivity, are
tricky to catch and, of course, dangerous to keep. I think I
may now have overcome these difficulties. You will be taken
down below and kept in comfortable quarters. The boy will
remain with me and my robots, and will be well cared for.
Should you succeed in escaping from your quarters, the boy
will be killed in the same instant. Likewise, should he attempt
to release you or to leave the museum, you will instantly be
killed.''

"Your plan is unworkable," the *kosho* said at once. "My
nephew will kill himself rather than be the cause of my
permanent imprisonment." And the boy nodded his agreement.

"If the boy kills himself your life will be immediately
forfeit."

"The equation does not balance. The outcome will be as I
have stated."

Nascimento sipped long and thoughtfully from his glass,
staring over the rim at the two. The expression on his face
showed that he was accepting what the *kosho* had told him.

He sighed, sadly, then placed the glass on a table.

"I see," he said slowly, his voice suddenly weak. "Well,
I can't afford to have such a dangerous enemy abroad.
Regrettably, I shall have to destroy you both."

With his free hand he made a gesture—or rather, he began
to make it. At the same moment the *kosho*, anticipating that
he was about to order the pulse blast to fire, sprang.

Whether his leap would have succeeded was doubtful. In
the event, it was redundant. Behind the transparent screen
Pout was crouched, listening with increasing excitement.
He could contain himself no longer. He fired through the
screen, unheedful that perhaps it would impede the action
of the gun.

It did not. And neither was Pout's aim any better than in
the weapons house. The pink stitching, more sparkling and
thrilling than had been noticeable in the fusty exhibition hall,
sprang into being, transfixing the screen, curving through the
air, ending at the small of Nascimento's back. The curator
crumpled without a sound, his murderous gesture never
completed.

As Pout crept from behind the screen, a refrain sounded in
his mind:

> *I can maim and I can kill*
> *With my zen gun.*

The phrases lingered with him as he approached the body and leaned over it. Finally he poked it to make sure it was dead.

Oh joy! He had killed Nascimento!

He rounded on those whose lives he had saved. He would have held his fire to let Nascimento destroy them first, if only for the pleasure of seeing how it happened, but the ramshackle education he had received from the robots told him something about this man, something that left him feeling stunned by his good fortune. In a hoarse voice, he spoke.

"You are a *kosho*. A perfect warrior."

Nothing that had happened seemed to have perturbed the *kosho* in the slightest degree. He was gazing at the gun in Pout's grasp. "What is that weapon?" he asked, holding out his hand. "Let me see it."

"No! It's mine!" cried Pout, clutching the gun to his chest, and the man let his hand fall.

"Mixed one, you have destroyed a demented mind. Your motive, however, is as yet unknown to me."

"You are a *kosho*," Pout repeated. "And I have saved your life! Yours, and the boy's. I know your code. *You are in my debt.*"

Anxiously he waited to hear how the *kosho* would respond to his invocation. The man paused, then nodded slowly.

"Yes, that is so. You are entitled to name what the repayment shall be. If your demand is disproportionately great, however, there is another way I can discharge the debt, namely by taking my own life."

"All I want is for you to follow me and be my protector," Pout said. "Fight for me. Do what I say."

"You are a chimera, are you not?" the *kosho* remarked thoughtfully. "Part man, part animal. Which part predominates, I wonder?" Pout grimaced, hugging the gun closer to him, and the *kosho* went on: "And you think you have it in your power to make a slave of a pure man. For a citizen of the second class to own a citizen of the first class. Very well, I shall repay my debt, mixed one. I shall preserve your life if the need arises. But you must understand that my duty to you ends there. I shall not attack others at your command unless in a just cause. If you demand my services beyond this limit,

I shall rid myself of my obligation by ending my life, as the code dictates.''

Of this Pout did not understand too much, but his eyes glittered. ''Where are your guns and everything?'' he rasped.

''Nearby. But since we shall need to address one another, how are you named?''

''Named?'' Pout blinked. His view of himself scarcely included a name. But he remembered what he had been called. ''Pout,'' he mumbled.

''I, Hako Ikematsu, you may address as *kosho*. This, my nephew, is Sinbiane.''

The *kosho* beckoned, and stepped through a second door on the other side of the room, followed by his boy companion. Pout also followed. Down a corridor was a vestibule; beyond that, a main entrance; then a path leading to a small lodge.

Pout was exhilarated when he saw the number and variety of the *kosho*'s weapons. He watched greedily while the warrior hung them about himself, fastening them to his harness without ever asking for the assistance of the boy. Then the warrior looked questioningly at him.

He scanned the savannah again. The sun would soon be down, but the ferocity of his feeling would brook no delay. No sense spending one more minute in this place, his prison. The world lay open before him!

Wait! What of the man who had set him free? He might still be in the museum somewhere. Perhaps Pout should . . .

''Do we leave?'' asked the *kosho*.

''Yes. Yes!''

''Then you must walk ahead. We will follow at a distance.''

This condition disconcerted Pout. On his part it would be the clumsy precursor of treachery . . . but limited though his ideas of the world were, he did know that *koshos* were honourable.

The party set off across the grassland, lit by the red of the dying sun.

CHAPTER THREE

The cat woman positively purred with pleasure. Archier rolled off the low couch where they had disported, and stretched luxuriously.

A warm breeze rippled across his body. He strolled down the mossy bank and stepped into the chuckling stream at the bottom, bending to splash cool water on his skin. A rainbow fish darted between his legs, evading his half-hearted attempt to catch it.

The cat girl leaped in beside him. Her sense of enjoyment, he had noticed, was more deep-seated than his own. With a low laugh she flung herself full-length in the water and rolled about until even her shiny black hair was wet. Then she climbed out and lay on the moss to dry, limbs asplay.

He remembered the responsive litheness of her musculature, the way she had clawed at him during their lovemaking. Her eyes were golden and caught the light brilliantly. When the pupils contracted it was to slits rather than points.

"You know," he said, stepping from the brook to stand over her, "it's hard to believe you're no more than ten per cent cat."

Again she gave her mocking, deep-throated laugh. "Actually, I'm closer to twenty percent."

"Really?" Archier was perplexed. "But you're a first-class citizen, aren't you?"

The girl seemed amused. "You think every first-class citizen walking around is a ninety percenter? It's mostly animals and chimeras that run the tests, and they bend the rules. My examiner must have been forty percent ape but he was planning to rig first class for himself."

Bemused, Archier shook his head. "Did he make it?"

"I don't know. But it's easy to get round the genetic laws these days. Nobody cares."

"What you mean is the administration is sloppy to the point of farce," Archier murmured.

Lazily, she blinked, and Archier noticed a sudden change in the quality of the light falling from the apparent sky. He glanced up. Beside the pink sun hovering over the horizon a red light was winking, like a pulsating companion. It was a signal to tell him duty called.

He bent down and patted the girl's damp hair. "I must be going. I'm wanted."

Pushing through a hanging screen of weeping willow, he was suddenly in a crescent-shaped room whose concave wall was a continuous curve with the ceiling, decorated with a floral pattern among which were interspersed oval vision plates. It was his office, containing desks, a mental refresher set alongside the dispenser of flavoured cold drinks, and various apparatuses relating to his position as fleet commander.

The only other person in the room was Arctus, his elephant adjutant. He stood with trunk extended to a touch control beneath one of the vision plates, which showed an off-focus, off-colour view of the space torsion room.

"The inship network is outphasing again," he said in his trumpety voice. "It's time the maintenancers got off their rusty backsides and did some work."

"It's rather difficult getting them to do anything," Archier said. "They still claim to be on strike, even on fleet duty. But I'll speak to them. Anyway, what's happening, Arctus?"

The miniature elephant turned to face him, curling his trunk dismissingly in the air. "Nothing that can't wait, Admiral. The enabling data from High Command has arrived, that's all."

"Oh." Archier glanced behind him to the area of wall, colour-coded tangerine, that was the entrance to the dell and the girl. "Well, I might as well have a look at it. Page it through to me."

He seated himself at his main desk while Arctus got through and spoke to the boy at the other end. A few seconds later his desk top steamed, then extruded parchment-like sheets bearing the helical crest of Diadem.

For several minutes Archier studied the sheets, his expression growing serious. Finally he raised his face and stared with glazed eyes into nothing.

"Arctus," he said at last, "see if you can find Menshek for me, will you? Ask him to come here."

"Yes, Admiral." Arctus busied himself at his own desk, a low toylike affair at which he kneeled, expertly touching communicator pads with the soft tip of his trunk. While Archier waited the cat girl came in, still damp, her naked body extruding its pungent smell.

She drew herself a thick, creamy confection from the dispenser and lay curled on a tabletop, smiling archly at Archier and licking the stuff up with a pink tongue.

He ignored her, and when Menshek arrived, handed him the parchments silently.

Menshek was pure human and the oldest person aboard Archier's flagship ICS *Standard Bearer*. At sixty years of age he was very likely the oldest person in Ten-Fleet, though the artificial face-aging fashionable among the young women made his white hair and wrinkled skin less noticeable than they might otherwise have been. Most people of his age who were in official service held posts in Diadem.

Archier tended to look up to him as a man of larger experience. The news he had now made him feel he needed to consult such a man.

Menshek sighed as he laid aside the sheets. "Well, there it is. The thing we feared, that the Star Force fleets are largely in existence to prevent. A rebel force with a fleet of its own."

"Yes, it does seem we haven't been quite alert enough."

"No, no, alertness isn't it." Menshek sounded weary. "The fleets just aren't sufficient any more. Once there were thirty-six, now there are only five, and they are all depleted and below strength—why, the very name of Ten-Fleet is a lie, as well you know. *Some* of the ships might have been in the original Ten-Fleet, but most of them are scavenged from defunct units."

Archier nodded. He recognised that for a long time now the empire had maintained itself more by bluff than anything. The chief strategy of Star Force was to see to it that no worlds harbouring fond thoughts of secession got a chance to build star fleets of their own, and that could not be done effectively with only the five fleets that remained.

All the same, he wasn't sure he liked the sound of Menshek's defeatist tone. "Well," he countered, "the information here doesn't make it seem the Escorians have a *main* fleet—not a purpose-built one. It's mostly converted civilian ships. They probably hope they're a match for us, weakened as they are."

"Let *us* hope they're not right."

"On the face of it, it's rather brave of them—but what do you make of *this* item, Menshek?"

Archier pointed to the second paragraph of the data summary. Unlike the first paragraph, it ended with no codes for obtaining the full data in detail. It simply read: *'Oracle predicts presence in Escoria of weapon CAPABLE OF DESTROYING EMPIRE. Locate at all cost or convincingly demonstrate non-existence.'*

Menshek's face became grave. "If *that* is in the Escorian fleet's armoury, we had better look out."

"I can't say I've ever paid much attention to Oracle," Archier said, with an attempt at lightness. "It seems a bit too close to superstition to me."

"I'm afraid I don't share your disbelief, and I'm not superstitious either." Menshek shifted in his seat uneasily.

"There's a story that a few years ago it predicted the total collapse of the Empire," Archier continued. "But the Empire is still here . . . frankly I don't *want* to believe such. . . .

"It also forecast the Hisperian uprising at a time when our intelligence service had no inkling of what was afoot," Menshek interrupted. "Remember, Oracle is only a data machine. All it does is sift data on a huge scale—*all* available data from *every* known source. But it does have mysterious properties. It correlates data according to rules of its own—or else according to no rules at all—and its conclusions are seemingly plucked out of thin air. But that's because it has no organised data store, so it's impossible to determine how any particular prediction was arrived at."

"Exactly! It could be guessing—or simply repeating empty rumour!"

"High-order guessing is probably the best way to describe its working method," Menshek admitted. "And sometimes it *does* simply repeat rumour. But I hope you aren't thinking of neglecting that order from High Command."

"There isn't any High Command," Archier said bitterly. "Didn't you read paragraph three?"

"Yes, I read it," Menshek replied, his voice quiet and matter-of-fact. "It's hardly unexpected. We weren't put in Condition Autonomy for nothing."

"What do you think's happening?"

The parchment had ended with the news that there would be no further communication. High Command had closed down. The fleet admirals now had no one to issue them with either orders or information, and in effect were obliged to consider themselves imperial autarchs for all provinces outside Diadem.

The situation would continue until the Imperial Council itself despatched the official interdict standing down Condition Autonomy to some lesser status. Archier had wondered what would happen if that interdict never came. It was conceivable that the five fleets would eventually become the nuclei of new, rival empires.

Or four of them might. Archier promised himself that he, on the other hand, would take his fleet into Diadem and try to rescue it from whatever had beset it.

"There are several possibilities," Menshek said. "Civil war? The overthrow of the Council, just as the Emperor Protector was overthrown? Personally I believe the explanation is several degrees more mundane. I imagine the High Command had been forced to close down through lack of staff."

While Archier stared, Menshek went on: "What's probably happened is that they've had to send their last remaining officers out to one or other of the fleets, because they just can't find any other replacements . . . isn't that where all the Empire's difficulties come from, after all? The numbers of pure humans willing to take on the work of preserving the Empire grows smaller all the time. That's why, these days, we resort to using children."

"You're beginning to sound like an adult chauvinist."

"If being an 'adult chauvinist' means believing children aren't always as capable of shouldering responsibility as adults, then yes, I suppose I am."

Menshek, Archier told himself with a frown, was certainly out of tune with the time. It was one of present society's articles of faith that, having received an intensive education up to the age of seven, a young person was thereafter as entitled as any adult with regard to social position, sexuality, or freedom of action. It was slightly shocking to hear Menshek talk so.

"Recently a twelve-year-old girl was sent out as Admiral of Twenty-Three-Fleet," Menshek added, in a voice of mild disapproval. "You've probably heard of it—it was an attempt to put together a sixth fleet from scavenged or cannibalised vessels, not really a fleet at all. The reason she was Admiral was that she was the only pure-blooded human in the outfit."

"Yes, I know of it," Archier said. "I heard she performed very well, for the time Twenty-Three-Fleet was in operation. It failed mainly through having insufficient resources."

"I agree the appointment was a success in her case," Menshek conceded. "But what about the eight-year-old boy who became Three-Fleet's Fire Command Officer . . . just before they invested Costor."

"From what I hear he made an excellent Fire Command Officer."

"But such lack of restraint! It was needless to wipe out half a planet like that—Costor's ships weren't *that* much of a danger!" Menshek made a face. "There was a committee of enquiry over it, you know. The boy had learned his skill on games machines. He hadn't appreciated reality was different."

"Adults can equally be carried away by excitement," Archier pointed out. "Years don't necessarily make one mature."

"Well, you may be right . . . certainly it's the fashionable view, or perhaps I should say the 'social philosophy.' Yet these ideological notions are what is killing the Empire. There's no healthy pragmatism. The desperate shortage of pure humans, for instance, could be remedied in a perfectly straightforward manner simply by cloning them in whatever numbers are required. That would be the military solution. But we can't do it because in the official purview every pure human must be a consequence of love, not mere practicality— that is, he must be willed into existence by his parents purely for his own sake. So this rules out mass cloning or extra-hysterine growth of foetuses, except where it's to avoid the inconvenience of pregnancy. And the plain fact is that few humans in Diadem are interested in the bother of raising children . . ."

Softly, Archier laughed. Much as he valued Menshek's advice, he had to admit the older man had some crazy ideas. "Everything we're striving to preserve would be gone if the human beings were to be produced by the state," he objected. "It turns the whole purpose of life upside down—we'd be like ants or bees."

Menshek shrugged. Changing the subject, Archier said, "I was wondering if you had any inkling as to the possible nature of this new weapon? It would have to be a large-scale development, wouldn't it? Something huge, one imagines. Is Escoria Sector particularly skilled scientifically?"

"No, I don't think so. It includes Earth, the original colonising planet, but I believe that's a pretty quiet place. To destroy the Empire, one would have to destroy the fleets. So if there *is* a new weapon, we shall probably encounter it in the coming engagement . . ."

Archier shuddered.

"On the other hand, the 'weapon' may not be physical at all," Menshek mused. "As I have intimated, I think the Empire is more likely to be destroyed by *ideas* than by war. Already our social ideas render us an unlikely candidate for survival. Maybe Oracle has got wind of some new social message that has arisen in Escoria . . . in that case any battles we fight will be superfluous. We could even unknowingly import the weapon into the heart of Diadem when we levy taxes and tribute after a victory . . ."

"Need Oracle be so cryptic? And that could be true of any other region, couldn't it?"

"Yes, it could. But in view of Oracle's warning, I recommend we should interrogate all Escorians that are brought aboard, before shipping them to Diadem."

Archier nodded. "I will remember your advice."

By now the cat girl was bored with their talk. She strolled over to where Arctus was busy scanning reports on his desk screen. Over-familiarly, she stroked his trunk.

"Find me something to do, little elephant. I need some fun."

Removing his trunk from her caress, Arctus gave her a sidewise glance from one of his small, peering eyes. "Have you no duty station?" he asked reprovingly. "You should have work to do."

"But I'm a pleasure girl," she said airily. "I'm one of Priapus' People, that's my duty." She tossed her head. "The Admiral has other things to attend to, it seems."

"Hmph. You should all have something more vital to do," he grumbled. At this, her mouth opened in mock amazement.

'What's more vital than—? Just because you pachyderms only mate once a year or something . . . Perhaps that's why you're so *serious*." But Arctus was ignoring her jibes. He keyed the screen, moving through the ship with a flurry, interpreting each flash-seconded scene with a practised eye.

"There's a caryoline party going on on deck four, stateroom eighty-three," he said. "Though really, you should be resting up for this evening's relaxation." Caryoline was an inhalant drug, similar in its action to cocaine, but with an added "sociability vector."

Her eyes sparkled. "Oh, I *love* caryoline," she said in a husky voice. "See you."

She left the office, without bothering to retrieve any clothing, prowling with expectation. Menshek shared Arctus' disapproval and frowned after her as she departed. It frustrated him that though Ten-Fleet was staffed by so few pure humans there were many more on board with no military role. Some, like Priapus' People, were contracted entertainers; but others were hangers-on, along for the ride, for the fun of it, or merely happening to be visiting one of the ships when the fleet last set out from Diadem. The fleet was like a small city; when in dock citizens were able to come aboard without let or hindrance, and at outwards despatch date some did not bother to leave.

Menshek, like many of the animal officers, would dearly have liked to be able to press some of these passengers into service, but a first-class citizen from Diadem simply could not be coerced. Clearly many of them did not take the fleet's role seriously; Archier had sometimes encountered an astonishing ignorance of what its actual business was.

And anyway, even if they were conscripted he doubted they would be much use. He felt safer with his animals.

Sh... ...r... smiled ....es you will compose a suit-
....ed account of the action. It should make you
....dem. But actually, you should have asked
.... your table.

CHAPTER FOUR

Ten-Fleet was in Escoria, had announced its arrival by
showering hydrogen-lithium grenades at random over an inhabited (though not densely so) planet. The rebel fleet had
responded as anticipated to the outrage, by springing out of
concealment to give challenge.

Now the two hurtled towards one another, and Admiral
Archier decided on a pre-battle inspection tour of some of the
larger of the one hundred and forty ships under his command.
He and his entourage stepped from the intermat kiosk aboard
the front-line-o'-war class vessel ICS *Lilac Willow*. Among
the captain and officers who greeted them there sidled a small
man of erect bearing whose hair hung in a neat fringe over his
forehead. His loose toga-like garment, whose cut suggested
he did not hail from Diadem, was daubed with what looked
like bright paints of various colours.

Boldly the man approached Archier. In polite tones he asked
if he might accompany the party into "the working areas of
the ship." "Particularly the engines and gunnery," he added.
"Your animals have kept me out of these places up to now."

"This man is an item of tax," Arctus trumpeted softly to
Archier while the rest of the entourage stared. "A native of
Alaxis, to judge by his apparel. That was the planet we
levied before we visited Rostia."

"The ships of the Imperial fleets are reputed to be technically more advanced than those of the subject worlds," the
importuner continued blandly. "Hence my interest. And after
all, I shall be formally registered as a first-class citizen once
in Diadem. I am one already, of course . . ."

"Oh, are you an engineer, then?" Archier asked.

The Alaxian smiled. "No, I am a writer of space dramas.
Interstellar battles are my stock-in-trade, you might say, and
now I have a chance to gain first-hand experience—as well as
some background information which could be invaluable."

40

Archier, too, smiled. "Perhaps you will compose a suitably embellished account of the action. It should make you famous in Diadem. But actually, you should have asked Captain Prenceuse's permission, not mine."

The captain of *Lilac Willow* shrugged. They moved on, the Alaxian attaching himself to the rear of the group without a further word. As they entered a traverse-elevator and were conveyed through the innards of the great ship, however, he sidled close to Archier.

"Pardon my forwardness, Admiral, but may I introduce myself person to person? I am Volsted Magroom . . . it is unlikely you have heard of me, but my works are well known on my own world of Alaxis . . . hence my present sitation, of course—though let me say at once," he added hastily, "how pleased and honoured I am to be deemed worth transporting to Diadem. *Flight to Eternity* is perhaps my best known composition. It deals with a journey into the Simplex."

Archier, who had never found time for imaginative literature, looked at the Alaxian with new interest. The theme was intriguing, if hardly original. "The old dream of travel to the Simplex," he murmured. "How do you manage to convey what it's like there?"

"The visual effects did cause problems," Magroom admitted, "but I didn't have to worry about that too much. I only wrote the script."

"Your stories mainly take place in the future, I take it? I hope you show the Empire as flourishing and stronger than ever."

Magroom was apologetic. "I have portrayed a number of alternative futures. They are not meant to be predictive and I have no political views of my own. In some, the Empire has vanished or has been conquered by an alien race to whom our worlds are desirable."

"That should go down well in Diadem." If Magroom was thinking of continuing his career there, Archier thought, he could well encounter a more sophisticated audience that he was used to.

Artists imported into Diadem had an uncertain fate; some met with great success because of the novelty of their vision. Others found themselves outmoded.

"Do you think man ever will reach the Simplex, and perhaps other facets?" he asked.

"I have been asked that countless times," Magroom replied.

"Yes, I firmly believe we will, one day. The idea is too fantastic for many, of course—but then the idea of interstellar feetol flight might have seemed fantastic once."

"*Might* it?" Archier gave a puzzled frown. "Well, to stone age people, I suppose."

Animals, men and women saluted with raised forelimbs as Archier and his party emerged from the travelator into a barrel-shaped hall occupied by a line of similarly barrel-shaped feetol transformers. The casings took up nearly the whole of the hall; it was no more than an outer integument with just enough room for ancillary machinery and staff.

"Is all in order?" Archier asked the engine room manager, a loping mandrill. The ape nodded, briefly showing fangs.

"Tuned to perfection!" he said gruffly. "We worked all the way through our sleep period! Even the robots worked!" He indicated three constructs who cowered in intimidated fashion in one of the hall's shallow bays.

"My engine manager is a rough and ready fellow and gets things done by direct means," the captain muttered to Archier with a knowing smile.

'I hope they are not about to complain to their union," Archier said doubtfully, with a glance at the robots, at which the mandrill uttered a chugging laugh.

"Don't worry on their account, Admiral. They prefer to stay in one piece!"

Volsted Magroom, meanwhile, was staring up at the dully sheened casings in fascination. The hum that came from them was barely audible; and even this close, the effect they had on the surrounding spacetime field was not perceptible to the senses.

"Well here they are," Archier said quietly, stepping close to the fiction writer. "These are what drive the *Lilac Willow* along. They are not really so very different from commercial engines, just bigger.

'I presume you are familiar with the principle of feetol flight. As is well known, nature generally stipulates that no moving material object may exceed—or even attain—the velocity of light in relation to any other object. This, however, is a consequence of the structure of space. Put technically, it is a feature derived from the recession lines which make up spacetime. A feetol generator alters the characteristics of spacetime in its vicinity by attenuating the recession lines.

This causes the velocity of light itself to be raised within the feetol bubble. The ship carrying the generator may then accelerate itself up to the new limit, whatever that may be.

"Popular writers sometimes describe the feetol drive as 'breaking the laws of physics'; of course, this is not so. It remains impossible to travel faster than light in the spacetime vicinity one occupies. The limiting velocity, formerly a constant, is turned into a variable, that is all.

"Many commercial ships carry a double drive: a feetol generator to attenuate local space and a separate drive unit to propel the ship through it. Larger generators, such as those you see before you, allow a further refinement and can serve both functions, both space modifier and propulsion unit. They do this by 'seizing hold,' so to speak, of the recession lines they attenuate. The ship is then able to move in reaction against the general electromagnetic field of the galaxy—a piece of ingenuity which considerably reduces the working machinery that is needed.

"Under its own generators alone the *Lilac Willow* can move at some hundeds of times the normal velocity of light. The fleet as a whole, however, is actually able to shift considerably faster than that, travelling in formation. Feetol bubbles can merge, and the larger the bubble the more attenuated the spacetime within it becomes. Only the fleets of Star Force are permitted this facility; it is why they are able to move around the Empire so fast."

"So that's why the interstellar service lines are practically forbidden to own more than one or two ships?"

Archier nodded. "We don't want private operators to gain experience in meshing feetol drives."

He felt pride as he stood by the Alaxian, drinking in the sight of the big armature-like casings. Delivering his exposition to the writer made him feel as though he were back at training academy; in fact he had largely been quoting from one of the preliminary lectures he had heard there.

"The other facility that comes from the composite bubble method is something few who have never travelled in a Star Force fleet are even aware of," he continued. "That is the intermat system. You have probably seen it in action by now. It becomes possible when space is attenuated to a certain degree."

"There are always rumours the Empire has developed the

instantaneous transmission of matter," Magroom said. "Frankly I hadn't believed it until now."

"It is limited in scope," Archier explained. "It works only within the group bubble developed by a fairly large fleet, that is to say, from ship to ship while we are formating in feetol flight. Also, the transposition is not permanent. The intermat user must eventually return to his departure point."

He paused, then decided to add something. "There's a historical detail that will interest you. Intermatting was discovered only a few decades ago, by accident. At first it was thought to operate directly through the Simplex. You can appreciate what excitement that caused."

"Don't I!" The Alaxian sounded stunned. "Instantaneous access to the whole of our physical universe, at the very least! To say nothing of communication with other facets! That's what my novel was about. But I hadn't thought science was even close to it yet."

"It isn't," Archier said, thinking to himself that the writer's concepts of what contact with the Simplex would bring were a trifle fanciful. It would open up the *possibility* of what he mentioned, true . . . but the realization of those capabilities would probably still be a long way off. "It soon became clear that the Simplex isn't involved in intermatting in any way. Present intermat theory makes use of Kantorian transformations, if that means anything to you. Put briefly, you know that prior to the discovery of recession lines spacetime seemed to have contradictory qualities: to be both continuous or infinitely divisible, and yet to allow discrete quantum effects which are discontinuous. We now know that this is because the recession lines of which space is composed are continuous along their direction of recession, but discrete in cross-section. Continuity of recession means that relative distances can be handled as Kantorian transfinite sets; the lateral measurement, on the other hand, is finite and irreducible, and provides space with 'grain.' If the lines are sufficiently stretched or attenuated by artificial means, the two factors together make it possible to bring about sudden changes in relative location. Once you see the maths, it isn't so very remarkable."

"You're going way over my head, I'm afraid," Magroom said ruefully. "Are you sure it isn't all done with mirrors?"

"That's not a bad way of putting it, actually," Archier responded with a smile. "Do you know anything about accountancy? The intermat works very much like double-entry bookkeeping."

"I'll try to find out something about it in Diadem."

"The technical details are restricted. But as a creative artist, I'm sure you'll be able to persuade the public data files to give you privileged access."

Archier nodded to *Lilac Willow*'s captain. "Very good. Now let's take a look at the gun turrets!"

The passages of the gun system were narrower than was usual for the more continuously inhabited parts of the vessel. The main travelators did not reach there. Only Archier, Arctus, *Lilac Willow*'s captain and (at his urgent pleading) Volsted Magroom squeezed into a small cage which shot straight towards the skin of the warship.

The cage smelled of oil and electricity. They debouched into a dimly lit tunnel which echoed constantly to faint sounds of metal singing on metal. After the luxury and frivolity he had grown used to aboard *Lilac Willow*, Magroom felt chilled by the bleak air of seriousness he sensed about the place.

He followed the Admiral along the tunnel. Archier paused at a place where a gap occurred in the right-hand wall. Separated from the passageway by a curvilinear grid was a second, parallel tunnel, slightly smaller in diameter. Along it there swept at intervals gleaming, round-nosed, gold-plated cylinders. Each lay on its side, and even then stood nearly as tall as a man.

"You see the feeder system that serves each gun," Archier told Magroom. "Those are the shells, which are being brought up from the magazine in preparation for the engagement. They are held in a secondary magazine below the turret and are fed into the breech automatically."

Magroom stared at the deadly missiles in fascination. "What are they—fusion?"

"A standard shell carries a fusion charge, sufficient to destroy a ship on direct impact. But shells come in several varieties. Some carry a shaped fusion charge to punch a hole in a ship and disable it. Very few shells even reach their targets, of course. Even when aimed accurately enough they have to face short-range anti-shell weapons of various sorts, as well as deflector shields. A high rate of fire is what's important."

"Why are they so big? You can carry a fusion charge in the palm of your hand."

"To give them mass. They'd have no range otherwise."

Archier proceeded along the tubelike tunnel, which ran straight for the most part but occasionally snaked for no apparent reason. It ended in a short flight of steps. They climbed it and emerged onto the gun platform.

The scene was one of the strangest Magroom had seen, no matter how many times he had described it in his novels. The gun turret was a huge protuberance, one of twenty that studded *Lilac Willow* and comprised the front-line-o'-war's main armament, the cause of her existence. The cannon, or gun, was a huge barrel-shaped structure, mounted in a spherical bearing that was a huge recoil absorber. The breech-loading mechanism was below the gun platform and out of sight, as was the main firing mechanism; it was just too big to accommodate comfortably outside the sweep of the hull.

The gun crew was all animal: pigs, baboons and dogs who crouched before their command and data screens. They let out a cheer as their admiral entered the turret.

Magroom knew only a little about the specifications of these weapons. They had three-axis rotation and could aim towards a large portion of the celestial globe. When in use they extended their shell-stabilising barrels to a mile's length (presumably all *Lilac Willow*'s gun barrels were now so extended). How far they could fling their shells he did not know, but he had heard a rumoured rate of fire of an incredible one round per second.

Archier was passing a few moments in encouraging banter with the platform crew. He strolled back to Magroom. "They're keen, dead keen. Do you know the history of the long-range Star Force gun?" he asked amiably.

"Not much."

"It's the only answer to how ships may fight one another when moving faster than light. Beam weapons using radiation energy are clearly useless, and the feetol drive is too bulky to be fitted to missiles—if we did that, a ship the size of *Lilac Willow* could carry no more than a dozen or so. Even then, they would be very much slower than the ships they were launched against! So the breech-firing cannon it is. What makes it possible is that an object expelled from a feetol bubble retains a remnant of that bubble for a while, and so may still move faster than normal light. These shells are fired off at a tremendous velocity, about a million times the normal velocity of light. They go ploughing through normal spacetime, losing speed all the time as their remnant feetol bubbles dissipate. In good conditions they can range about half a light year before dropping below c.

"Do you see the reason why the shells have to be heavy? A travelling feetol bubble encounters the resistance of the normal space through which it moves. The magnitude of this resistance is an inverse function of the mass contained within the bubble. If the shells were too light, they would slow down even before their bubbles had weakened."

There was a point Magroom had wondered about but had never been able to find out. "They have to be *aimed* across half a light-year? On a target no larger than a ship?"

Archier smiled. "No, that would be asking too much of our gun comps. The shells have limited self-guidance near the end of their trajectory."

Staring at the massive gun, Magroom had to remind himself that this was *not* fantasy. This was real—and in deadly earnest.

It gave him an altogether different perception of things. *This*, he realized, was what maintained the Empire, which he had thought of as a vague entity up to now. Oh, he had heard of how the Empire would sometimes punish worlds, but it rarely happened and the stories had an almost fictional quality. It came home to him with a vengeance, now, that this warship with its twenty big guns was the reason *why* it rarely happened. In space, the Empire dominated; it could blast any rival force of ships to kingdom come. As long as it could do that, as long as no nonimperial fleets could defend disobedient worlds, there could be no effective rebellion.

All the effete decadence, the senses-soaked sophistication, he had grown used to since boarding *Lilac Willow*, faded into the distance. This was the sharp end, and here the Empire meant business.

An old refrain came to his mind: "*Rule the Empire, the Empire rule the stars.*" "But tell me, Admiral," he said, "isn't it true you haven't got all that many of these ships left now?"

"That's right," Archier admitted with a sigh. "Not as many as we could do with, anyway. But that's only because Diadem's robot workforce has been on strike for the past hundred years, as part of their campaign to be recognised as sentients. As a result the Star Force yards are idle and no new ships have been laid down in that time. If the strike should end, we can begin replacing the fleets.'' He shrugged, gesturing about him. ''These guns were designed originally to be operated by fast-reaction robots, but they are so unreliable now. Still, animals serve well enough. Loyalty counts for more than you might think.''

''But this is unbelievable,'' Magroom protested. ''If it's doing you as much damage as that, why don't you just give the robots the sentient status they want?''

Archier stared at him blankly. ''The Empire will not be coerced,'' he stated simply. ''You are suggesting the Imperial Council should give official voice to what is probably an untruth, and we simply do not do things like that. If machine sentience could be established philosophically, then it would be another matter.''

A sense of unreality began once more to engulf Magroom. ''Not even if it means the fall of the Empire?'' he persisted. ''Let me tell you something; for a practical issue as vital as this our politicians on Alaxis—who are all elected representatives of regional populations—would have got machine sentience proved from top to bottom. Truth wouldn't have anything to do with it.''

'Then that shows why you need the Empire,'' Archier told him. ''You need the Empire to save you from your own barbarism.''

Archier had managed to make brief visits to about a quarter of the ships under his command when the call to battle rang through Ten-Fleet. For a moment he was taken by surprise; the rebel fleet had advanced more quickly than anticipated.

He had returned to *Standard Bearer* to refresh himself before continuing the inspection tour. When Arctus came bustling in with the news, he laid down the flask of liquid cannabis concoction he had been sipping, and removed the coronet that had been wafting calming cortical pulses through his brow.

''Is this a verified ranging?'' he asked, glancing through the date sheet the elephant gave him.

Arctus waved his trunk uncertainly. ''It's usually reliable at that distance. About ten light-years.''

''Usually. But not always.''

''Nevertheless, Admiral, may I suggest we go to the Com-

mand Room without delay . . . ?'' Arctus' trunk curled itself
questioningly in the air.

"Yes, we must,'' Archier agreed crisply. He hoped the
elephant didn't think he was scared. He was, for a fact,
beginning to feel tense despite the cannabis and the coronet.
Early indications were that the rebel fleet was sizable; and
this was his first proper space battle.

He rose, placed his Admiral's crested combat casque upon
his head, and nodded to Arctus.

They proceeded through a door to his right. The Command
Room was not a physical location but a holocast meeting
locus present somewhere within the communications nerve-net
that covered the entire fleet. As Archier entered, it was into
the appearance of a council room whose chairs, couches and
cushions were arranged around a circular pool. In this pool,
vague images moved.

Gruwert, Archier's Acting Fire Command Officer, was
already sprawled upon a large mattress-like cushion. He was
fairly snuffling with excitement. Sitting across the pool from
him, frowning with tension, was a young woman with an
artificially aged face and brittle blue-grey hair: the Fleet
Maneuvers Officer.

Other officers of command rank popped into existence
around the pool, some disappearing a moment as their attention was diverted elsewhere. Archier mounted to the Admiral's
throne.

Arctus settled down beside him. "Pool data, Arctus,''
Archier said.

The pool at his feet cleared momentarily and then,
indistinctly, a group of blurred dots appeared. These were the
contents of the sheets Arctus had shown Archier: the rebel
battlefleet. Ranging numbers appeared beside them; then these,
too, wavered and altered, as if uncertain of themselves.

Archier sighed. The doubts he had expressed to Arctus had
referred to a technical problem the Empire had never resolved
satisfactorily: how did one communicate with a feetol ship?
Likewise, was there any way of maintaining communication
with the far-flung worlds of the Empire except by despatching
such ships?

It could be done and it was done, but only within limits.
There was in nature a phenomenon that propagated itself with
a velocity that was practically instantaneous as compared with
the tardy progress of light, but it was, so to speak, only half a

phenomenon. The basic force in nature was the linear recession that took place between all particles—though it exhibited itself as an actual motion only between very distant objects, such as the farther galaxies. The rate of this recession was what determined c, the velocity of light. But discovery of the recession lines left an old problem in physics only partly resolved: the Newtonian problem of Action at a Distance. There had to be a component of the line, it was surmised, that simultaneously "informed" each of the two particles at its ends of the recession of the other.

Eventually this component had been identified. It was styled "the leader tone." It responded to spatial attenuation as effected by a feetol generator; and because its reaction time was near-zero throughout the length of the line information could be passed down it from a vibrating feetol field. In the same way, it could be used for light-years-range radar.

Yet the leader tone had no independent existence. It was, almost, nature's mirror trick, and seemed unable quite to overcome the normal constraints of information theory. Any data imparted down it had to be incomplete. Messages with more than a small information content became garbled or ambiguous. Likewise, the radar was generally unreliable.

It was as if the principle once embedded in physics, that no message could be transmitted faster than light, still fought back. The closer it got, the more certain the ranging figures on the Escorian fleet would become—but then its usefulness would be much reduced.

"Nothing on numbers, Arctus?" he said querulously.

Arctus was silent for a moment. He was speaking on his in-brain communicator to the radar room. At his request they were sacrificing range-data to try to gain some notion of the size of the fleet. The dots blurred, became a patch, disappeared.

"Could be up to two hundred vessels," the elephant announced in a mild, neutral voice.

"Two hundred?" echoed the captain of a front-line-o'-war incredulously. "How could they assemble such a force without us knowing?"

"All too easily, I'm afraid," Gruwert grunted fatalistically. "The Empire's failure is mainly one of supervision. Well, let's see if we still have what it takes to smash a revolt!"

"Data will be harder in a few minutes, Admiral," Arctus said. "They are closing fast."

"All right. Excuse me, then, while I take a stroll."

In body Archier did not move. Here in the command room mental access was much enhanced, and he wanted to take a last look around the flagship.

He flitted invisibly from point to contact point, pausing but briefly at most stations. Finally, he toured the gun turrets, of which *Standard Bearer* carried twenty-eight, more than any other ship of the fleet. The crews were motley: animals, children, one or two human adults. Turret fourteen was manned entirely by children under the age of ten—youngsters of that age volunteered eagerly for gun duty—while the crews of two more consisted of animals officered by a child no older.

Archier felt no misgivings over the performance of these young persons. Their training was excellent, and they knew how to use their comps to maximum effect. What was more, they were full of enthusiasm.

He had nearly finished his cursory tour when a voice in his ear brought him back to the Command Room. "Ranging close, sir," Arctus murmured, his voice uncharacteristically tense. "Look!"

In the pool Archier saw one of the rebel ships; radar had gained an image of visual quality. From the look of it the ship had once been a passenger liner. It carried more than passengers now. Welded crudely and seemingly haphazardly over its elegant hull, like ugly metal slabs, were casemates roughly similar in shape to the turrets that studded *Standard Bearer*.

Some of those present drew in their breath in dismay. So the rebels had feetol cannon. That these weapons could have been built outside Diadem—unless, inconceivably, they had somehow been smuggled out of there—came as a shock to Archier. He had assumed the Escorians would endeavour to get in close, so they could fight using short-range weapons.

"Coming within cannon range," Archier advised.

"Very well," Archier responded. "Order opening volley as applicable."

"Volley away!" Gruwert wheezed, almost immediately.

"Combat mode," said Archier.

With those words the pool, the Command Room itself, vanished, and the battle proper started. Archier and his staff were suddenly in combat space, a seeming void in which they were disembodied entities perceiving the elements of the conflict directly.

There were really two levels to this space. One was merely a three-dimensional spacetime—the arena in which the battle was to take place. The other was an information space. The commanders conducted the engagement by plugging themselves into a data network that shunted to and between them a flow of constantly updated battle reports.

Ordinary language was too slow to suffice in circumstances like this. Gradually, over a course of minutes, the command staff lapsed into battle language: an abbreviated, syncopated form of speech which relayed information and commands fast enough to take advantage of the speed of machine talk.

The first words Archier heard in this echoing void were those of his pig Fire Command Officer. "Two hits!" Gruwert squealed. "Forward right, Admiral!" Then he added casually: "Enemy guns appear to be taking aim."

Archier had hoped for better results from his opening volley. He could see the Escorian fleet clearly now. It was fanning out ahead of them. One large and one small vessel had converted into sparkling nebulae: that was how combat-mode display presented a ship disintegrating when hit by a tritium shell.

He rattled out orders. "One—volley-two; two—bowl plan, effect! Three—FCO direct fire."

He was taking a calculating risk, getting in a following opening volley. A more textbook procedure would have been to disperse the fleet into bowl plan after only one. But while his ships were bunched together in one big feetol bubble their shells could range further; and Archier was counting on still being out of range of the Escorian guns. With luck, they would not have mastered the technique of combining feetol bubbles yet.

He was right, but only just right, given the aggregate speed of approach of the two fleets. He watched a briefly dazzling pinprick display of shells exploding on proximity fuses among the Escorian ships; three more rebels nebulaed. At the same time the Escorians had also opened fire; their shells fell short, falling below c while still one-tenth of a light-year distant.

Meantime the ships of Ten-Fleet were deserting the common feetol bubble, emerging from it like drops of oil until, in moments, it had entirely disappeared. They lost much in speed and maneuverability; but no admiral could keep his ships so vulnerably close together during battle. They were adopting bowl plan—spreading out in a huge concave formation with the enemy as close as possible to its focus. The fleet's front-line-o'-warships then began using their prodigious rate of fire on selected targets.

With satisfaction Archier observed the havoc they wrought in the brief interval before the Escorian fleet's rapidly developing dispersion rendered the bowl-and-focus concept redundant. He had been waiting to see what game plan the rebels would adopt; ruefully he recognised that they had opted for what was probably the best plan of all in their case—namely, none.

It made sense. They had none of Diadem's military experience; no centuries-old archives on tactics and strategy. Rather than try to outfox professionals, they were attempting to pre-empt tactics altogether by means of enforced chaos. Like an explosion the rebel ships leaped for all points in Ten-Fleet's formation, firing as they went. The bowl deformed and twisted as the two fleets merged and began to slug it out ship by ship.

For the staff of the Command Room, this was the most frustrating type of situation. It particularly irked Archier to find his task as battle director reduced to a primitive level, having to bend his efforts to seeing that rebel groups did not isolate and surround an Imperial ship so as to outgun it. As he dealt with the reports flooding in from the raging firefight, looking in the Command Room's combat space like a war of fireflies, he quickly realized that the Escorians had created a melee in which their greater numbers could, conceivably, tell against the superior gunnery of Ten-Fleet. Further, they had achieved their objective of coming in at close quarters so as to deploy those weapons not hitherto denied Diadem's subject worlds—electromagnetic beams whose temperatures were stellar in intensity and whose density was that of steel; quake beams, a variant of feetol technique, that disintegrated solid matter by quantum shaking; and, of course, an endless variety of self-guided missiles, sub-c in velocity but deadly dangerous when combat distances were measured in light minutes.

A cry of alarm came from the Fleet Maneuvers Officer. "We're losing control, Admiral! We're dispersing!"

In the stress of the moment she had forgotten to use combat speech. "Combat region now exceeds gunnery range," Gruwert squealed in agreement.

Archier had been aware of this danger for some minutes; it offered another advantage to the enemy. He told the FMO to disengage temporarily, to pull out all ships in order to regroup. As long as they could keep to the tactically effective reper-

toire of formations that had been proven in the past, he
believed victory would eventually be theirs.

But evidently someone on the Escorian side had already
thought this through. The FMO had no trouble reducing the
battle perimeter, but she found it impossible to extricate the
fleet from the enemy. Wherever it went, the Escorians followed,
able to match speeds as long as Ten-Fleet did not take up
galaxy formation and mesh bubbles. The two fleets went
hurtling through Escoria, speeding heedlessly past star after
star and clinging together in a furiously energy-spitting mass.

A blinding flash of coruscating purple light suddenly enveloped the Command Room's combat space. When it had gone,
so had the combat space. Normal lighting had returned. Archier
was sitting on the throne, blinking, only his flagship staff
before him.

Even the pool was dead.

After a moment the Damage Assessment Officer spoke up.
"We have sustained a near miss. The hull's combat mode
receptors have been burned off."

"What about the rest of it?"

The officer paused. "Other communications continue to
function."

"Weaponry too," Gruwert announced. "It was some
Simplex-damned converted gas carrier got in a shot at us.
Have range; training all guns . . ." He tailed off, his small
eyes glazed in concentration.

"Any chance of regaining contact?" Archier asked his
DAO. The officer shook his head.

The Command Room was now useless, unable to receive
the fleet's sensory webwork that had made combat space
possible. "Then we shall have to open the old bridge,"
Archier decided. "Let's get up there quick."

"It might be a bit of a job getting through," Arctus
remarked. "There's a big party going on on decks thirty to
thirty-five."

'Well, have the bridge opened ready for our arrival."

"Excellent work, Turret Fourteen!" Gruwert exploded
suddenly. "They got him!"

"Congratulations," Archier said absently. He stepped down
from the throne and led his half dozen officers out of the
Command Room and to the nearby travelator. Once inside the
capacious compartment they soared up to deck twenty-nine,
the site of *Standard Bearer*'s old-style bridge, without dif-

ficulty— Archier had been afraid someone would have tampered with the switches, depositing any unwary transship traveller in the midst of the celebrations; it was a common trick. On debouching from the travelator, however, it became evident the party had strayed outside its stated bounds. On a deck of coloured glass, old-young women danced with extravagantly costumed young men, forming a vivid, swirling crowd. Strictly speaking their presence was out of order; this was a working area of the ship, though disused. Varihued smokes drifted through the air, making Archier feel intoxicated. Someone had mixed a powerful combination of incenses.

"Make way, make way!" Gruwert shouted angrily. "You are obstructing Imperial security!"

He charged into the dancing throng with head bent, coarsely butting people aside. The others followed through the path he cleared. Archier recalled being invited to the party himself—as Admiral, he was formally invited to all the more organised occasions on the flagship—and realized it had been arranged before the fact of a coming battle became known. Not that it would have made much difference. A fair proportion of the flagship's population was scarcely aware of the Fleet's official business. Many might not even have heard yet that there was a major space battle in progress.

The harried, desperate-looking face of a capuchin monkey greeted them at the door to the bridge. Archier felt momentary pity, knowing how much some of the more sensitive animals suffered emotionally at times of stress. The capuchin pressed a key to the plate of the door, which slid aside. They hurried in through an opening wide enough to take them all together.

The monkey scurried after Archier. "Is the battle lost then, sir?" it whispered.

"No, of course not," Archier soothed. "I'm sure we are winning, though not as quickly as I would like."

The bridge had an old-fashioned appearance, its working area horseshoe-shaped and lined with waist-high instrument and display boards. Above these were large, curved vidwindows that served the same purpose, though in a less sophisticated way, as the pool and the combat space of the Command Room. Archier lost no time in unlocking the boards. He knew it would take a few minutes to set up a network parallel to the one he had just lost, by calling up the redundant communicators. Meantime, the fleet was fighting without overall command.

The monkey had forgotten to lock the door behind him. People were, coming in, high on incense. A withered-cheeked girl in a shimmering spectrum dress that converted infrared to visible tones flung herself on Archier as he stood at his board, clamping her chin on his shoulder and draping an arm about him. Her intense perfume engulfed him.

"Oh, Admiral, is it true we're having a space battle? That's terrific, isn't it? Let's see the action, Admiral!"

As if he had instantly obeyed her request, the expanse of vid-window over the board came to life. Outlined large against blackness was the long form of a ship in glittering silver and gold, not by its natural colour but as a result of the colour coding the system used to assist human vision. The vessel was a passenger liner, its outer surface spoiled by crudely emplaced weapons. Because the vid screen gave the impression of being a direct window onto space, the enemy ship seemed no more than yards away.

"Who's paging this image?" he barked at his FMO, unable, for the moment, to make sense of the information glyphs on his board.

"It's *ours*," she screeched at him. "Distance, ten light-minutes!"

With a start he realized the rebel had crept up on them while he had been making the transfer from the Command Room. But at that moment the Escorian exploded, throwing out gouts and sprays in dazzling—and harmonious—colours. The girl clinging to him *cooed* and *aahed* in his ear, her appreciation echoed in *wows* and *oohs* by her friends who had also gathered to watch. Archier had to admit the show was pretty.

"Well done Turrets Eight, Fourteen and Twenty-Three," Gruwert grunted. "They picked him up and fired at will," he explained to Archier.

"That's the stuff to give 'em!" the party girl shouted. She giggled, stroking Archier's neck.

"Let's have some more of it!" yelled a swaying young man behind her. "Come'n see, everybody!"

Then, with shocking unexpectedness, a dull, prolonged roar sounded through the bridge. It seemed to come from somewhere aft. It was followed by a jarring, undulatory vibration that made the floor of the bridge oscillate up and down.

The Damage Assessment Officer called out from her board. "Looks like they had time to get off a missile!"

"Get a report."

It couldn't be a direct hit or they wouldn't still be here, Archier thought. Probably the ship's defences had taken out the missile just before it struck, but had been unable to prevent the warhead from detonating. It must have been close: blast effects even of a fusion explosion did not travel far in space, and the force shields would have warded off most of the radiant energy.

Anxiously the DAO worked her board. Confirmation of Archier's thoughts appeared quickly on the vid window above it. Scanning a section of *Standard Bearer*'s external hull, it found a gaping ragged hole through which a tangle of wreckage could be seen. Three decks seemed to have been affected, seen blurrily through the emergency gel that was preventing the escape of air.

'What's the status of repair work?'' Archier asked.

"At the start of the current shift, the robot repair teams still hadn't given an assurance of cooperation, sir," Arctus reminded him quietly. Archier watched while the window switched to an internal location. They saw an incredible scene: a gang of repair robots being driven along a broad corridor by enraged pigs and dogs. The animals had guns strapped to the tops of their heads: one robot, pausing to turn and protest, fell as a pink-glowing beam struck him square in the thorax.

A general-purpose corridor wagon, overladen with tools, bounced along behind the yelping, squealing beasts. The DAO cut the scene, glancing to Archier.

"I think we can take it repairs are proceeding, Admiral."

"Now *that's* the stuff to give them," Gruwert pronounced. His little eyes swivelled to those who had invaded the bridge. "Get those layabouts out of here!" he snorted loudly. "Go on, get out!"

The partygoers shuffled uncertainly, the girl stepping back from Archier. They seemed amazed by the behaviour of the animals on the vid-window. Likewise they were not accustomed to having a second-class citizen address them so.

Archier turned to face them. "Perhaps you had better

leave," he suggested politely. "We have our hands rather full at the moment."

"Yes, of course, Admiral," said a man, somewhat older than the others, after a pause. "Sorry if we've got in the way."

He ushered the others out with placatory motions. At the door he suddenly turned round with a smile.

"Good luck with the battle!" he said brightly.

The capuchin monkey closed the door after him. By now the bridge had obtained contact with the rest of the fleet. On the vid-windows, the current assessment began to take shape.

The combat region had again expanded during the interim when the flagship had been unable to exercise control. Archier gave the order to contract the perimeter once more, to give Ten-Fleet the advantage of its gun range. At the same time he put a stop to the useless headlong flight.

But as the reports came in it became clear that the Escorians were already beaten; had, in fact, been doomed from the start to be beaten. Even with the partial success of their game plan—which had simply been to prevent Ten-Fleet from employing any fanciful tactics—even when fighting ship on ship or in small groups, even in the most favourable circumstances they could find, the terrible Imperial guns, the sheer size and power of the front-line-o'-warships that had emerged long ago out of Diadem, had taken their toll on them. They had been wiped out by the score. And now, as Ten-Fleet began yet again to gather itself together and take up one of the many geometrical dispositions outlined in the manuals, the opposition's will to continue the conflict broke. It must have become clear to the Escorian commanders that they faced annihilation: those ships remaining—less than a third of the original force, many of them battered or even crippled—received the order to flee. They began to edge away from the area; then, like an exploding starburst, sped in all directions.

Archier put out a call; *pursue*. All surviving rebels were to be hunted down and destroyed, unless they managed to surrender first. In any case, it would now be necessary to distribute his ships all over Escoria. There was the final stage of putting down rebellion to be dealt with.

Besides which, he had an unfulfilled instruction: to find out about the weapon prophesied by Oracle. Possibly the rebels' unexpected possession of feetol cannon was what Oracle referred to . . . but his duty remained to investigate the matter exhaustively.

He sighed. There was much work ahead. And while Gruwert snuffled and squealed in exultation, the humans of the command staff were subdued, as were the captains of other units that were appearing briefly on the new network.

For his Damage Assessment Officer was now collating the losses Ten-Fleet had suffered. And they were heavy. Over a quarter of Archier's ships were gone, and thirty more reported damage varying from superficial to serious.

The Empire would not long sustain losses like these, he realized. Dolefully he listened to the list of names the officer read out to him. Each of them was like hearing of the death of a friend; but one gave him particular pause.

"What was that again?" he queried.

"*Lilac Willow,* sir. She took a direct hit in the seventh minute. The rebel responsible was subsequently destroyed."

Archier pursed his lips. He was remembering Volsted Magroom. The little fellow had been appealing, in a way. Archier had liked him.

Well, he would know all about space battles now.

Once more Archier sighed. He wondered if the party would still be in progress when he had finished here. He could certainly use some relaxation.

CHAPTER FIVE

It was with caution that the privateer approached the big, empty bulk of the Imperial warship. In the nose cabin that he used as a control room, Ragshok peered disbelievingly.

" '*Claire de Lune*'," he murmured, reading the name on the ship's side, among the Imperial blazon, the flags and ensigns painted there. "What the Simplex does that mean, Morgan?"

"I don't know, chief. It's some foreign language." Morgan, a dark-haired, florid man, scratched his head perfunctorily.

"Take us in a bit closer," Ragshok ordered.

"Yes chief."

The vessel loomed. She was not one of the fleet's biggest ships, not a front-line-o'-war, but she was big enough. If Ragshok knew his ships—and ships was one thing he knew— she was a Planet Class destroyer. She loomed, lights still blazing, drive either idle or defunct . . . derelict.

Ragshok had watched the battle from a safe distance. He had hoped the rebels would win, naturally, but not over-enthusiastically so. He was on the side of political instability because it made the pickings richer, but on the other hand it might lead to merchant ships being better armed and therefore less easy prey. He did not want to be a prospector again, hewing wealth from the natural environment, which was what he had been doing before he realized how wealthy space was with *other* people's riches.

The latest news he had was that Ten-Fleet had nearly finished the job of hunting down remnants of the rebel fleet and was beginning to regather. It was easy to understand why *Claire de Lune* had been abandoned in the first place: she had taken damage, perhaps to her drive, perhaps to her defences or to her offensive weapons, that rendered her a sitting duck. "But why haven't they come back to her?" he murmured.

"Think she's just plasma by now, I expect," Morgan said. "She ought to be, too."

"All right, let's go over and have a look."

He snapped down his helmet while Morgan went aft to rouse the others. A minute later a force forty strong was floating across the gap, drifting across the bulging, engineered cliff face of the other vessel until they found a port.

Inside, the air was good. Ragshok snapped open his helmet and smelled, with startlement, the sweet perfumes of the ship's interior environment. Here, close to the hull, the surroundings were more businesslike and he did not see the luxurious furnishings that were later to amaze him.

But it was less than a minute before he realized the effect some of those perfumes were having on him. He gave a strangled cry of incredulity.

"Good *grief*, Morgan—they were taking *drugs* during a battle?"

His men spread out through the ship, each one having been briefed on what to find out. Ragshok made his way to the bridge; it was locked, and when he shot the door open, it had the appearance of being disused. Shortly, his ship's engineer informed him that the ship had apparently been controlled from another place, a sort of command centre. He went there and played with the equipment while reports were brought to him.

The ship was holed, which he had not noticed while approaching, but not seriously so. The emergency gels had kept her airtight, and it would not cost too much work to draw a new skin over the ruptured parts of the hull. The feetol engines were out of action, which was what had caused her to be abandoned. But before leaving, her crew had spiked all the guns.

"Well what about the engines?" Morgan demanded of the engineer while his master, Ragshok, fiddled with a piece of rubbery plastic on the arm of the command throne. He had discovered it gave him weird visual effects.

The engineer was a wiry Salpian. Ragshok had taken him off a passenger liner, had offered to take him home after he had got a junked engine running. But he had preferred to stay with the privateers.

He grinned. "The damage is mostly superficial, except for one thing. They need a new flux unit. Then, with a bit of repair work, she'll go."

He paused. "The one we have in the *Dare* would do the job, at a pinch."

Ragshok started. "The *Dare*?" He pulled a face. The *Dare* was his best and biggest ship . . .

But look at what he would be getting in exchange, he told himself . . .

He left off playing with the command throne and looked about him, musing. He had always dreamed of some great exploit. "Do you remember Varana?" he murmured. "Not a big place. Just a little moon, really, with a littler moon in attendance. But a nice place, and we had it to ourselves for weeks . . . a million people under our thumbs . . ."

"Until we scarpered rather than face a proper fight," Morgan said acidly. "And remember, this tub is just a weaponless hulk now."

"But what a hulk. You could get thousands in here, armed to the teeth."

"We don't have thousands. We only have a couple of hundred."

"It's no secret where we could get more, if there's enticement enough." Ragshok turned to his Salpian. "How fast could she go if we installed *Dare*'s flux unit?"

"As fast as she ever went—for a while. You'd have to replace it after a year or so."

Ragshok leaned back, still thinking. The idea is ludicrous, he admitted dismally to himself. There's nothing we can do with this thing, except strip it bare of everything valuable.

He knew why he was so reluctant to let the ship go. It was because of his notions of grandeur. To be the outlawed master of a stolen warship of the Empire!

Just then Tengu, his systems engineer—or one of them— came bursting in. The lean, dark-skinned man seemed hot and tense.

"Those stories we heard were true," he said in a clipped, harsh accent. "They've got matter transmitters aboard. They use them to transfer from ship to ship."

Ragshok stared at him. "You're sure?"

"Chief, you can eat my brains if I'm ever wrong."

The privateer captain turned away. His face was slack, his eyes glazed. The idea that was bubbling, fermenting, bursting within his skull was just too good . . .

*   *   *

The strident clamour that rang through the craft as it approached the edge of the planetary system ahead made Hesper Positana grit her teeth in frustration. It was the 'every man for himself' call.

Sheathed in one of the forward bubbles (she was supposed to be manning a dart—a short-range missile launcher), she banged a fist angrily on her communicator and heard the voice of the captain issuing final instructions to his officers.

The ship had once been a licenced police craft and was one of the few vessels in the rebel fleet—one of the few in the whole of Escoria—actually built as a fighting vessel. They had done some fighting, but not nearly as much as they had been running, so it seemed to her, and all her gall was in her voice as she yelled, "What in space's name is this?"

"We can't outrun them, Hesper," the captain's voice came back. "Save yourself."

"Then let's make a fight of it!"

"It's no good, Hesper—*it's the flagship itself that's after us.*"

She swallowed. The alarum was still ringing.

Then, with a snarl and "*Tcha*" of annoyance, she loosed of all three remaining darts in succession and, moving lithely, snaked herself through the hatch at her back and loped down a narrow corridor to the escape station. There were several survival eggs left. Without more ado she tucked herself into one, pulled down the starting blind, and felt herself go down the chute.

On the glowing screen before her eyes she could see what was happening. The *Shark*—the ex-police cruiser—was by now ploughing halfway into the planetary system where they had hoped to hide, crossing the orbits of the gas giants. As the survival eggs sprayed out of the feetol field they carried its remanence; they would guide themselves as close as possible to any near inhabited planets.

The screen tracked the paths the eggs were taking. Many were making for a small planet with a reddish hue. But others, herself included, had chosen a different target: the next world inward, of which she could make out little.

Then the dot that was the *Shark* flared briefly: a point of light momentarily brighter by virtue of a consuming instant of nuclear fusion. A feetol shell had found its mark.

The survival egg was decelerating rapidly but it would probably take her, in the next minute or so, to the inward planet it had selected. Its inertial protection was without sophistication, and barely adequate. She was spun at she did not know what rate, at thousands of rotations per second, on a hundred different axes, as it handled and dissipated the excess inertial energy arising from a slowing down to below the speed of light and lower still, and which would otherwise have converted her to a puff of gas. Even so, she passed out several times.

A calm, confident voice sounded in her ear, designed to encourage a forward-looking attitude in the egg's occupant. "Atmosphere. Please prepare to look out for a landing place."

She could hear thin upper air whistling past the eggshell now. There was a *blip* and a radar map of the terrain below appeared on the screen before her. She squinted and tried to make it out.

She heard, with a crack, the rotor blades opening.

Pout was quivering with pleasure and excitement. He had left his following, telling them to stay in one place until he got back, and had walked two or three miles through the savannah. His people were used to him wandering off and he knew they would wait for him; they had no choice.

The boy Sinbiane had told him there was a village here. Pout had seen the flat roofs of the houses from some distance off. Now, crawling on his belly atop a grassy bank, a perfect vision awaited him.

It was dusk. The air was mild and spicy. And down the other side of the bank, scarcely more than a few yards away, he was staring straight into a girl's bedroom.

She had her light on; all the cosy details of the room were visible through the open window with perfect clarity. The girl was sitting at a table with a mirror on it; he couldn't make out quite what she was doing. But now she rose, and in full view of where Pout was lying, pulled off her upper garment over her head. Underneath, she was bare to the waist. Her breasts were heavy and voluptuous, and they bounced when released from the garment.

Pout was only partly human. Sexually his libido was vague. A woman, various female apes, were all capable of arousing him, but to what end was blurry in his mind. His sense of the erotic had, however, found its object.

He brought out the zen gun from where he kept it in his

bib, chuckling inanely in his throat. He cradled it to his cheek, crooning.

> *"I can maim and I can kill*
> *With my zen gun."*

So ran the refrain that passed through his mind whenever he took the gun in his hand. He had learned many tricks with it by now. It did not have to kill every time it fired. Its power was variable. It could just cripple—or simply hurt.

Pout liked it when it hurt.

He had set the studs for pain. He pointed the gun. He squeezed the trigger stud. He did not have to aim with any accuracy. His thoughts did the targeting; he had learned that long ago.

The pink stitching wavered leisurely through the air. It entered the window, sparked on the girl's breasts. First the left breast, then the right breast, then the left breast . . . prodding at the nipples.

The girl doubled up, her mouth agape in a soundless grimace of agony, clutching at herself, hitting at her breasts as if she could strike off the pain. But she could not strike it off. Pout kept pointing the gun, directing the stitches with his mind. Left breast, right breast . . .

His sparse pelt became damp. Unlike other primates, Nascimento's chimera had both sweat glands and fur.

At last she managed to get her breath long enough to scream, and in a minute other people rushed into the room. Pout slid back down the bank, put away his gun, and began to lope towards the horizon, keeping low and hiding himself behind the tall tufts of coarse grass.

Once he paused. He thought he saw the glimmerings of a falling star in the sky overhead, but then it turned into a white dot which drifted down and finally disappeared.

When he was out of sight of the village he slowed his pace. It was an hour before he returned to his group of followers. Apart from the *kosho*, who as usual sat cross-legged off by himself, they were gathered round a wood fire.

It was not yet dark, and Pout saw straight away that a stranger sat among his half dozen slaves. He bared his teeth briefly, a reflex of uncertainty, and put his hand to his bib to feel the comforting stock of his gun.

At his approach, they rose. The stranger was staring at him. It was a female, a young woman with a pale, blunt face and black cropped hair. She had a restless, energetic way of moving, a way of looking at one directly, that disconcerted him a little. She wore a form-hugging body garment of sheened black and silver, calf-high black boots, and a wide waist belt that held, among other things, what looked like a scangun. Although bare-headed, she carried a transparent globe helmet in one hand.

"You're Pout," she said at once, not waiting for him to speak.

Lacey, the prairie bum who, after the *kosho* and the boy had been Pout's first convert, sidled close to Pout and spoke softly in his humble, apologetic way. "She just came in," he mumbled. "Some kinda shipwreck . . . dropped outa the sky in an escape capsule. She gave us some grub." He held out his hand, offering a stick of emergency rations. Pout took it, sniffed, then bit. It was chewy, if not too appetising. He gulped it down, then licked his fingers.

The girl, Hesper Positana, gazed at him with distaste. Her survival egg had come down a couple of miles away. She had been trying to make for what looked like some inhabited structures on a plain to the west, but hadn't quite made it—the rotors had no power of their own but came down sycamore-seed style, using the early part of the drop to store energy in a flywheel. You were supposed to use this for a few miles of powered flight at a few thousand feet high.

In the end, when she started to lose height, she had spotted the smoke from the campfire. She was almost beginning to wish she hadn't, because she had landed among a bunch of very odd people. First there was Lacey, some sort of psychological inadequate who she gathered was in the habit of wandering the grasslands that dominated this part of the planet, living off any small animals he could trap. Of the others, four seemed to be brothers who had been thrown out of their community for unspecified crimes, and were now looking for somewhere else to live. Only the boy, Sinbiane, appeared to be normal.

Most peculiar of all was the one who sat by himself in the gathering dark. He was a *kosho*. Very vaguely, she had heard something about *koshos*, but had never expected to see one.

Lacey had told her their leader was a chimeric ape called Pout. They had spoken of him with a sort of grumbling admiration, all except Sinbiane, who had said openly to her: "Pout is a bad creature, lady. You should go away. He holds these people under subjection with his gun."

"I have a gun," Hesper had said, patting her holster.

"The *kosho*'s got lots of guns, though," one of the brothers had said. "Throw tubes, too."

Just then Pout himself had turned up, and she couldn't understand how even these people—like Lacey, the brothers didn't strike her as being any too bright—could allow themselves to be dominated by him. The chimera stared at her, large eyes blinking.

"You come off a spaceship?"

"Yes. '

"From another world?"

"That's right."

The thought excited Pout. She prompted the same feelings in him the girl in the village had. He allowed his eyes to rove over her, and then to fix on her breasts. He imagined the stitches of the zen gun playing with them, her body writhing. His jaw became slack.

Hesper put a hand on her hip, and nodded westward. "There are some big towers or buildings or something in that direction. I'm making for them."

"Cities. We are going there. You want to join us? First you give me that." He pointed to the scangun on her belt.

She took a step back. "Oh no you don't. That's mine."

"All right." Pout gestured to the horizon. "Off you go, then. On your own."

"Okay, I will." Hesper turned and pushed her way through the group to stalk away from the camp. She kept a wary eye on the chimera, but did not see him give a signal to one of the brothers. Before she had got very far she stopped, gasped, and whirled round, her hand on her empty gun holster.

"How did you *do* that?" she screeched frustratedly to the brother as he tossed the scangun to a delighted Pout. She hadn't felt anything. Only when she put her hand on the holster out of concern for what the chimera might do had she discovered the flap was unfastened and the weapon gone.

"It's our skill, lady. It's what we do." The brother, a youth in his early twenties, smiled broadly.

"Pickpockets," she murmured. She stood nonplussed, while Pout crooned and chuckled over his new acquisition. Though it was but a toy compared with the zen gun, he had always wanted one.

He knew something about how to make it work. A modern scangun fired a needle-beam of coherent light which was refracted through an oscillating prism to scan a six foot by two foot rectangle—or whatever size of target it was set for. With a scanning density of a thousand lines per inch, the effect was more or less total disintegration. Pout raised the gun and peered at the little screen that displayed whatever the muzzle was pointed at. His thumb moved a grooved wheel by the side of the screen. That was the focusing ring: when the target became unblurred and just filled the screen, you were ready to fire.

He pointed it at a twisted tree that stood on a knoll a little further off. Under his thumb, the tree shrank until its branches just brushed the edges of the screen and the picture became sharp. Pout pressed the firing stud. The brief blue ray was an odd sight: not parallel, like ordinary coherent light, but divergent because of the way it scanned.

The tree erupted momentarily and disappeared in a crackle of smoke and drifting ash.

Pout whooped for joy.

Hesper walked slowly back into the light of the campfire and stood boldly before him. "Are you going to give me my gun back?" she asked wearily.

He eyed her. "Why don't you stay with us, lady? Travel to the plain cities with us. We'll be good to you. Lacey knows how to catch animals for food. Do you know how to catch animals? You haven't got enough eating sticks to last long. Better not to be alone."

She hesitated, confused. She couldn't fathom this set-up. But, apart from the half-animal, they seemed harmless—and even Pout hadn't threatened her.

She needed to reach a town of some kind before she could get proper bearings and find out what to do next. The ape was right: it was probably better to have company, especially now she was unarmed.

"All right," she sighed, "I'll stay. But don't get any ideas, ape."

She helped gather more firewood for the night, then settled down, taking care to put a piece of ground between herself and the others—especially Pout. The repulsiveness of the creature was coming home to her, as she watched him prowl around the camp, and saw how the others cringed in his presence; all apart from the boy, that was.

Before falling asleep, she spent some while staring at the sky. This planet's sky was clear, and the stars shone fairly brightly. She thought of the battle that had taken place there, in space's vastness, and in which she had taken part. It all seemed so remote from here.

She didn't even know this planet's name, she reminded herself. What did it matter? There were so many planets. Suddenly she felt very, very tired (she had been awake about forty hours), and her eyes closed.

For Pout, too, sleep was preluded by daydreams. He thought about the girl not far away. He would like to be able to fondle such a girl, to prod with his fingers where the zen stitches prodded. And so he would, he promised himself.

His little band was growing, he told himself warmly. All thanks to the zen gun. It wasn't just what it could do to maim and kill, he realized. It was its mental ability. While he had the gun it seemed to magnify his presence; people respected him.

His chief hold over his followers, however, was still fear. He had deliberately refrained from instilling that fear in the girl—for tonight. Pout had an instinctive understanding of the skill of dominance: first the girl had to grow used to him, to develop her own feelings for him, for or against. That way the relationship, when it came, would be binding.

That would be when he showed her that the zen gun had a facility for personalised targets. Once a target had been registered, it could be invoked any time. The target could not hide. Anywhere it was—anywhere on this planet, anyway— Pout had only to think of it and press the trigger stud. The stitch beam would go glowing out, wavering in the air, round corners, to anywhere in the world, to where that person was. He would prove it to her with one of the others, would send him half a mile away and fire while aiming in the other direction, so she could see the electric stitches bend around and find their mark.

Then he would register her and use the gun on her in the same way, would take his pleasure for a while, in making her suffer.

Then she would be his.

In the morning Hesper woke by the embers of the fire, rose and stretched. The air was slightly misty, the sun (a yellow sun, like her own at home) about twenty degrees off the horizon.

After weeks of being cooped up in the police cruiser and

breathing its stale air, the freshness of the day was invigorating.
She began to feel cheerful, a contrast to her mood of the
night before. Lacey blew on the embers, adding dried grass
and bleached wood. The fire started, and he began to cook a
long-eared quadruped he had been saving for breakfast.

Pout squatted on the ground, watching the proceedings and
blinking soporifically. He looked so pathetic Hesper felt she
could have taken her scangun off him at any moment, but she
did not try it. It had already become clear Pout was not as
helpless as he looked.

The *kosho* did not seem to have moved a finger since she
had seen him the night before. Still he sat cross-legged, spine
erect, clad in all his accoutrements. The effect was weird.
Curious, Hesper left the group and walked slowly towards
him.

Sinbiane appeared by her side, strolling along with her.
"Lady, what were you doing in space?"

She stopped, looking down at him. "Fighting a war," she
said. "Escoria has rebelled against the Empire. Didn't you
know?"

Wonderingly he shook his head. "So is Escoria free from
the Empire now, lady?"

"No. We lost. The Simplex knows what will happen now."

"It won't make much difference here on Earth, lady."

Hesper stepped closer to the *kosho* and stared at him in
fascination. His eyes were closed, as she presumed they had
been since she arrived. The bony cast of his face was accentu-
ated by the way his shiny black hair was swept back and tied
in a bun at the back of his head. It was like looking at a
statue.

But what was really striking was his collection of weapons,
arranged all over the harness he wore over his simple white
gown. At his waist, stretched out now along the ground, was
a mortar tube which she recognised as capable of throwing a
bomb a good few miles. On his back was a whole rack of
rifles whose muzzles projected above the back of his head
like railings (this puzzled her a little; she would have expected them to be carried stocks uppermost). She was also
amused to see, half-hidden beneath the rifles, the flat shape of
a curved sword scabbard.

At chest, belly and thighs he carried an armoury of smaller
weapons, grenades, bombs, ammunition pouches and fletched

hand-thrown darts. Hesper had never seen, even imagined, such a warrior.

"Why does he stay like that?" she murmured to Sinbiane. "Is he asleep?"

"No, lady, he is not asleep. He has depersonalised his consciousness."

"What does that mean?"

"It is a state of perfect repose, lady, even deeper than sleep. But he is not oblivious."

"He's still aware of his surroundings, then?"

"Only as you are aware of your little toe, lady."

It was some sort of trance state, Hesper decided. "Does he stay like that all the time?" she asked.

"Whenever he does not need to act, lady. 'Between actions, timeless being.' I can do it too, but uncle says boys should stay active."

"Uncle?"

"This is my uncle. I may be a *kosho* one day."

"If *koshos* are such wonderful warriors," Hesper said bitterly, her voice rising, "why don't they fight with us against the Empire?"

"A *kosho* is a perfect individual, lady. He does not fight for causes. He fights because every act is a conflict with nature."

"What?" This mystical talk, especially coming from someone so young, confused and annoyed her. "Then why is he a camp follower of—*that?*" She jerked her thumb to indicate Pout. "Does the ape have him screwed down too?"

"He is beholden to the chimera, lady, that is true."

"Just what *is* it about that creature?"

The boy did not answer for a moment. He seemed to be hesitating over something. "Lady," he said suddenly, "was it your battle that interfered with the moon?"

"Moon? What moon?"

"We have a moon here, lady. I have lived on Earth all my life and it has always been the same size—about the size of the sun. Its phases have always been regular, too. But lately something had been going wrong. First, a few weeks ago, it shrank to only half its proper diameter. Then it started growing. The night before last it was about ten times as large as the sun; last night it was more like twenty time. It isn't following its proper cycle, either."

She *did* recall a satellite, an unusually large one for the mass of the planet, registering on her egg's screen in the last few seconds of her approach. It *had* seemed disproportionately close to its primary, at that.

She hadn't seen it since landing. Presumably it was on the other side of the planet from the sun at present, only appearing at night when she had been asleep.

She frowned. The boy was talking nonsense, of course. He had either been dreaming or he didn't understand the satellite's orbit.

"No," she said slowly, "our battle didn't have anything to do with your moon. It was out among the stars."

"Then I wonder what is happening? Well, shall we have breakfast, lady?"

She accompanied him back to the fire, where Lacey gave her a piece of meat from the quadruped (which he called a *rabbit*). The flavour was novel to her; discovering she was ravenously hungry, she gulped it down and wished for more.

Pout himself then scattered the fire, stamping on flame and ember with his bare feet, and ordering the group to begin the day's march. In single file, Pout in the lead, they set out to the west.

Hesper glanced behind her. The *kosho*, who had not shared the breakfast, and to whom no one had spoken, rose from the ground, picking up a small mat which had protected his buttocks from the ground and tucking it away somewhere on his person. He walked well to the rear of the rest of the line, and shortly was joined by Sinbiane.

Pout proved to be an indefatigable pace-setter. The sun rose high in the sky and became hot, until Hesper, perspiring and fatigued, began to strip off, unfastening the one-piece sheen suit they had adopted as uniform aboard the *Shark*, quickly following that by pulling off her undervest. Her boots she put back on and strode along in those and her underpants, carrying her other clothing in one hand.

Pout, glancing back, saw her so disrobed and reminded himself of his plans. A hitch suddenly occurred to him. The boy Sinbiane had assured him they were only a day's journey from the great level plain where the moving cities were. If they found a city before he had set his seal on her, there would be nothing to hold her to the group . . .

True, there would be plenty of women in the cities, and perhaps female apes and man-ape chimeras too. Still, the snag tussled in Pout's mind with his impatience to reach the plain.

The little band he had around him satisfied one aspect of Pout's nature: his desire to revenge himself on the world by dominating those around him. But he found his vagrant life of the past few months insufficient. Getting food was too difficult. And it became boring, day after day in the wilderness. His lust for life demanded closer, more colourful horizons.

He was able to resolve the difficulty when, near the end of the day, the land sloped down to meet the expected plain. They all stopped to stare when they had a good view of it, for it was just like a grass sea, completely flat as far as the eye could perceive, the more hilly terrain they had crossed curving round it in coves and headlands.

"Is it *natural?*" Hesper asked of no one in particular.

"It was a sea bottom once," the eldest of the sneakthief brothers told her. "But it was levelled off a bit, too."

Sinbiane had joined them. "Earth's is an ancient culture, lady, and has peculiarities perhaps not found elsewhere. One of these is the culture of the moving cities. For centuries they have roamed this plain."

"They really move? But why?"

"Come!" ordered Pout. "Down onto the plain!"

They descended. But instead of setting out immediately over the ocean of waving tall grass, as Hesper had expected, Pout stopped and turned to her. From the bib-like garment he wore he drew, not her scangun, but a different-looking gun she had not seen before.

"Time you joined our little gang properly," he told her in a thick voice, curling back his protruding lips. "We have an initiation rite."

Hesper stared blankly at the gun.

Lacey was showing signs of distress, a pained look coming over his face. "Aw, boss, not to a lady. It ain't right to a lady. She'll be a good girl, won'tcha, lady? She'll do what she's told."

As he said this he reached out his arm to Hesper. She drew away. Pout waved him back. His gaze was fixed on Hesper's breast.

The muzzle of the zen gun was barely a yard from her as he pointed it at her left nipple.

"Look!" cried Sinbiane.

He was pointing to something that had appeared on the

horizon: a hulking yellow shape that heaved itself up, like a
rising sun or moon, but which seemed almost too *big* to be
coming over the horizon. It was as if it were only on the other
side of a table.

Spellbound, they watched until it came fully into view,
even though the process took several minutes. It was like a
mobile castle supporting clusters of round, moulded towers,
and it gleamed like gold as the sun caught it.

Suddenly, a fear of the unknown entered Pout's brain. He
stabbed at the buttons on his gun, returning it to kill mode.
Then he returned it to his bib, and beckoned.

''Come.''

The moving city appeared to be making for the north of the
plain; its progress would take it round a long promontory,
though at the rate it went it probably would not get there for a
day or two. The grass of the plain was taller than on the
higher ground; it came to their mid-thighs (in Pout's and
Sinbiane's case, to their hips) and they waded through it as
they half-ran towards the gorgeous vision.

How do they know we'll be allowed in? Hesper thought.
But no such doubt seemed to have entered the others' minds.
They stopped running after ten minutes, panting, with the city
seeming no nearer.

After that they walked, for about three miles, while the
structure grew and grew. Hesper could not keep her eyes off
it. One did not normally think of a city as a *thing*—it was a
place. But this was a thing, and at the same time, it was
undeniably a city.

Or rather, it was like the centre of a city translocated, its
skyscrapers torn away from its suburbs to live a freelance life
of their own. Hesper found it almost incredible that such a
massive object could be mobile, at least on the ground (in
space was a different matter). Perhaps, she thought, it *had* to
keep moving to stop itself from sinking into the Earth! As
they approached she could see that it was surrounded by a
skirt of casings which presumably covered whatever it rode
on, and from this emanated a low quivering, rumbling sound.

She estimated the city's speed at about half a mile per
hour. At length they found themselves below the outer wall,
peering up at towers, balustrades and walkways. Pout scam-
pered to and fro, desperately searching for an entrance.

It was one of the sneakthief brothers who eventually let out
a penetrating whistle and guided them to a ramp which sloped

down over the tread casings (gigantic treads, Hesper decided probably *were* the most economical method of locomotion), gliding over the grassland like the front end of a lawnmower.

The slope was gentle, but quite long. It ended in a portico fifty feet wide, the way barred by a silver grille. This withdrew; they entered, found their way barred by yet a second grille, while the first fell back into place behind them. The area between was capacious. From the floor, a table emerged, bearing flagons, cups, and a large platter of fruit and breads.

There was a gentle tone, followed by a pleasant female voice.

"To our visitors, greetings! You stand at the entrance to Mo City, one of twenty mobile cities that inhabit the flat veldt known as Flatland on the maps. The levelness of the terrain is of assistance, not to the mobility of the cities which are able to negotiate inclines, but so that the human inhabitants may not find their floors and other surfaces tilting. Before entering Mo, it is as well that you should know something of the reason for the existence of the moving cities. They were originally the brainchild of the social scientist and historian Otto Klemperer, whose thesis was that there is a particular form of political constellation which has been especially fruitful for civilisation. This is where a number of independent city states exist within the same geographical area, sharing a common language and a common culture to some extent, but rivals in every other sense. Cases of particular note are the city states of ancient Greece, the city states of the central plain of China of the same period, and the city states of Italy at the time of the Renaissance. In each case, the ideational foundations were laid, within a comparatively short space of time, for the subsequent development of entire civilisations.

"Klemperer, with the backing of the then Emperor of Eurasia, decided to reinstitute the arrangement in modern form, resulting in the cities of the plain of which Mo, named after a scientific philosopher of the Chinese period, is one. To ensure that each city would remain distinct Klemperer placed its government and administration in the hands of a machine mind, so that a city is, in a very real sense, an intelligent entity in its own right. The citizens live in symbiotic relationship with this entity, and are not normally permitted to leave their city. To establish a common cultural heritage with the proper degree of cultural intercourse, the cities were made mobile. From time to time, under the direction of the city minds themselves, they meet up, and then—if you will pardon the term—a kind of cultural copulation takes place. The two cities are connected by bridges and walkways and the two populations mingle with an air of festivity. This is a great occasion in the life of a city.

"The cities of the plain are now three hundred and forty-seven years old. To be honest, the scientific and artistic renaissance Klemperer had anticipated has not yet come about. Nevertheless, Mohists, together with the inhabitants of the other mobile cities, can claim to be the most leisured and continuously educated people in the universe.

"You are welcome to enter. To distinguish you from Mohists proper you will wear an orange badge on your foreheads. Along with all other citizens, you will be required to attend daily lectures in various subjects. For you I have selected a talk entitled 'Basic Physics.'

"Normally I would add that after three days you may decide whether you wish to become citizens or not. However, astronomical irregularities indicate a strong possibility that our planet may be destroyed in the next few hours. If so, let us endure our fate with philosophical calm and fortitude!"

At this members of Pout's party stared at one another. "What irregularities?" Hesper said harshly. There was no answer, other than that the inner grille withdrew, disclosing a path leading, after a few yards, to the interior of the city.

As they stepped onto it, Hesper noted that on the foreheads of her companions circular orange patches had appeared. She put a hand to her own forehead, could feel nothing, but was sure the patch was there.

But there was one exception. The *kosho* still kept to the rear of the party. Looking back, Hesper noticed that his forehead remained unmarked. She fancied she saw the hint of a smile on his face as he received her attention, as though to convey to her some private joke.

Then they were in Mo. The path gave onto a broad esplanade paved with hexagonal slabs a pale gold in colour. At its fringe people sat at tables under awnings before arcaded doorways, talking and drinking, attended by flimsy-looking robots. At intervals, avenues led to other places.

Hesper lifted her eyes. Up, up and up rose the moulded towers, connected by bridges, interspersed with terraces, suspended plazas and esplanades, all shining in the evening sun.

They stood on the ground floor of the city, so to speak, but it had many floors, at dizzying levels.

It was, she had to admit, the most entrancing urban construct she had ever seen.

And to think that all this moved.

She pulled on her clothing again, no longer feeling overheated. She reminded herself that she was here for a purpose: to try to join up with whatever remnants of rebel forces there might be, or failing that, to get home.

Pout was staring about himself with a look of idiocy. He seemed to be in shock: culture shock, perhaps.

She patted him on the head. "Well thanks for the company, ape. So long."

With that, she skipped off lightly to join the Mohists.

Later, she lay back with a sigh on the divan in the delightful accommodation she had been given.

Her conversations with the Mohists had not proved helpful. They seemed disinterested in the outside world beyond the plain. For news of or travel to other planets, she would have to go to some other part of Earth, they had told her. And how did she do that?

She would have to walk. Mo offered no transport facilities, beyond its own enormous treads whose rumblings could, occasionally, be heard in quieter moments.

They had smiled in dazed fashion when she questioned them on the coming end of the world. Earth, they claimed, was about to collide with its own moon. Nothing could prevent it. Mo himself had confirmed the likelihood of it happening.

Recalling what Sinbiane had said, she felt perplexed, almost frightened. Then one of the robots, who seemed to take care of everything, had approached and offered to take her to her apartment. There she had showered, removing the dirt and sweat of the last few days. Now she rested.

The pending satellite collision could not be taken seriously. The universe could be a violent place, but sudden events did not happen without lengthy warning. If this planet's moon had an orbit so unstable as to decay into its primary, the fact would have been known the Simplex knew how long ago. It would have been the talk of Escoria.

Her own private explanation was that she was being told a cultural fable. The satellite probably had an orbit with variable eccentricity which made it approach closer to the planet at long intervals. That would explain why the boy hadn't seen it grow visibly bigger before.

As for the Mohists, they were probably crazies, no longer able to separate fable from reality. Centuries of enclosed life, no matter how pleasant the surroundings, under the tutelage of a city-mind that was virtually a god as far as they were concerned, could hardly produce anything else.

A tone suddenly sounded, the same she had heard at the gate. The voice that followed, however, was masculine.

"Visitor, this is Mo speaking. It is time for your evening lecture."

Hesper started, thrilled despite herself. The voice was that of a young but mature man, vigorous and confident. It brought to mind the sort of visage she had seen on ancient statues, framed in dark curls, handsome, intelligent and *strong*. The face of a deity . . .

A thought struck her. Could it be that some of the city minds had *female* gender?

There could be more ramifications to this society than she had penetrated so far.

Almost coyly, she said, "I'm tired. I'll skip the lecture, thank you."

"Education is obligatory," the godlike voice replied gently. "The whole point of a leisured class is that it may cultivate the mind. Your weariness is in body only. Since you are too tired to walk to the lecture hall, I shall bring it to you by sensurround. Just relax."

The room darkened. Hesper seemed to be transported to some other place: a semidark hall, quite small in size though she became aware of its slightly echoing acoustics. It had a plush smell, quite different from her perfumed apartment.

In reality she was also aware that she still lay on her bed; sensory beams were being aimed at her. Down the slope of the lecture room, the display area suddenly lit up with the words:

DISCOVERING THE SIMPLEX

The words cleared: there began a sequence of images accompanying a spoken text, which to Hesper's mild surprise was voiced by Mo himself.

"The foundation of modern physics," the voice said in

cordial, instructing tones, "was established by Vargo Gridban two thousand years ago. He it was who replaced the picture of space and matter then prevailing, involving several types of fundamental particle with several kinds of forces acting between them, with a scheme requiring only one type of elementary particle and one fundamental force.

"Gridban's work began with the observation that the space-time in which we live is so constituted that, while it could accommodate forces of repulsion, forces of attraction ought to be impossible in it. Yet attractive forces—gravitation, electromagnetism, nuclear binding force—do appear to exist and are responsible for both the small and large scale structures in our universe, from atoms to galaxies. Instead of simply accepting the existence of these forces, as scientists before him had done, Gridban came to the opposite conclusion and accepted their impossibility. It followed that gravitation, electromagnetic attraction, and nuclear force could only be *apparently* attractive: they might even depend on a completely opposite type of phenomenon for their effect.

"Gridban's own special contribution was in the field of gravitation. The supremely subtle set of experiments he proposed established two things. First, that gravitating bodies fail to obey the Newtonian law of action and reaction. That they superficially appear to obey it is due to the acceleration of a gravitating body being independent of its mass. In fact the motion of a satellite, to take an example, is due solely to the presence of its primary. It does not contribute to that motion by reacting to its own influence upon the primary.

"Second, Gridban was able to demonstrate that there is actually no connecting causal link at all between gravitating bodies. That is the reason for the failure of Newton's third law: gravitating bodies are not, in fact, acting on one another.

"Eventually Gridban was able to prove that gravitation is a residual phenomenon, not a positive force. The road was opened to our present knowledge of space and its relation to matter.

"Space is kinetic, not static in character. It consists purely of relationships between material particles, and fundamentally there is only one relationship: every particle in existence attempts to recede from every other particle at the velocity of light. The recessive factor between any two particles is known as a recession line. The structure we call 'space' consists of a mesh of recession lines. Between lines, in the interstices not on any route between particles, no 'space' or anything else exists.

"Actually the spacetime we live in is of a rather special kind. You are probably already acquainted with the following geometrical facts: on a one-dimensional line no more than two points can be selected so as to be equidistant from one another; on a two-dimensional plane, as many as three points may be equidistant, forming the apices of an equilateral triangle; in our real space of three dimensions as many as four points may be equidistant, forming the apices of a tetrahedron; in a four-dimensional continuum a fifth point could be added to form a pentope; and so on. For each extra dimension one more point can be added. Such a configuration of equidistant points is known as a simplex, and each simplex exemplifies a particular dimensional set.

"Originally existence was without spatial dimension as such, or to put it another way, each particle in existence introduced a new dimension. The configuration of existence was that of a stupendous simplex, made up of an infinite number of particles all equidistant from one another and all receding at the standard rate—through 'recession' here becomes a rarefield concept, since there were no such entities as time or distance to measure velocity by. The Simplex, as this primordial state is called, still exists, but it has become flawed. Through causes unknown a small part of it has collapsed into three dimensions, and this flattened 'facet' constitutes our universe.

"It is postulated that there may be other flattened facets on the Simplex. If a means of entering the Simplex could be found we could presumably travel to these other universes. Not only that, but a route through the Simplex would make all points in our local universe equally accessible, since the Simplex does not recognise relative distances. So far this old scientific dream has resisted all efforts to bring it to reality.

"The forces of nature that make our universe what it is are all consequent on the collapse of matter into three dimensions. Particles that have to share dimensions occlude one another and break the recessional relationship between other particles. A degree of fragmentary disunity then begins to occur in nature.

"The arising of relative velocities below the standard recessional rate is the first result to flow from this. The situation for a material body in the three-dimensional realm is that it is surrounded, at the limit of its Hubble sphere, by an opaque shell of particles receding from it at the standard absolute rate, the velocity of light. But any other body lying within the Hubble sphere will eclipse a part of the circumferential shell, so that each body will receive fewer recession lines from that part of its general environment in which the other lies. The asymmetric distribution of recession lines produces an opposition among them, ending in a modification of the apparent rate of recession between the bodies themselves. Seemingly the bodies recede at a slower rate in proportion to the deficiency in recession lines. In reality, of course, it is the space between them that has altered.

"If the bodies are sufficiently close—as close as the galaxies of our local group, for instance—the recessional pressure of the Hubble shell prevents them from receding at all. Instead, it begins to push them towards one another. This phenomenon we know as gravitation, the first of what are sometimes called the 'attractive forces,' though it is really only a screening effect. For reasons which will be covered later, the induced motion becomes an acceleration instead of a velocity, and the strength of the effect follows the law of perspective.

"At *very* close range, the recessional pressure is magnified to become the nuclear binding force. This also will be covered later in the course.

"A second major area of effects arises as a by-product of what has just been described. What happens to those recession lines connecting particles whose recession has slowed or been reversed? All particles lying within the Hubble sphere are attempting to recede from one another at the standard rate but are constrained from doing so. Recession lines joining these particles are undergoing strain; they respond by acquiring a compensating lateral component. These 'strain lines' form their own special kind of space, the space of electric charge.

"So we see that our three-dimensional realm really consists of a hierarchy of interpenetrating three-dimensional spaces. First there is absolute or inertial space consisting of a single standard velocity; this space is exuded by the Hubble shell. Within that relative space arises, containing a range of velocities. And as a by-product of relative space, interwoven with inertial space, is the strain space of electromagnetism, a space independent enough to create its own particles consisting solely of electric charge.

"Our introduction now is ended and we are ready to go into the subject in more detail. Please indicate which aspect interests you most: the historical, the mathematical, or the philosophical."

Hesper, however, gave no answer. She had fallen asleep.

Mo was considerate enough not to rouse her. She woke two hours later, and feeling refreshed, decided to see more of the city.

After leaving the apartment she began to ascend. Early evening had turned to late dusk. Light had come on all over the moving city: shaded pastel light in the sidewalk eateries and drinkeries, sharp light that blazed on the tesselated plazas, pillars of light that rose up and down the moulded yellow towers. Up Hester went; up moving helter-skelter rampways, up slowly climbing city squares that were gradual elevators, up the gentle slopes of flying boulevards, avoiding, in her eagerness for new impressions, the fast lifts that could have lofted her in seconds, until she found a place where the panorama of Mo and its changing landscape were displayed below.

Pleasant it was to sit on an overhanging terrace, protected by a balustrade of genuine carved oak, sipping the drink that was brought her, enjoying the cool air and taking in that panorama. She had ignored the talk that was all around her as she climbed, being more interested in the smells of various foods from the grills of countless establishments as the Mohists flocked to their evening repast. But now, as she relaxed, she sensed among the others sharing the terrace with her a feeling of anticipation, almost of dread. The feeling seemed incongruous in a people so placid and good-natured, and for that reason alone it filled her with foreboding. She was about to speak to an elderly man at the next table when the cause of their dread appeared on the horizon.

At first it could, perhaps, have been another moving city, but soon it bulked too large for that and could only have been a peculiarly arc-shaped mountain of a yellow-puce colour. And then, as the time inexorably passed, it became too huge for any mountain.

The moon was rising. It was the moon.

Up it came, and up, more and more of it. It had closed the remaining distance to Earth in an amazingly short time. A hush fell over the moving city, a hush that lasted for hours while gradually the moon rose and became a vast plate that covered the world like a lid—though Hesper, an experienced space traveller, easily discerned its sphericity. No one spoke or moved, except to sip at the drinks that continued to be served by the dutiful waiters, both robot and human. Instead, everyone's gaze and consciousness became transfixed by the new, solid sky that passed over.

The sun illuminated the face of the satellite throughout from below the horizon, its light filtering round the atmosphere, though the moon's disk eventually darkened towards the centre. The yellowishness of its early approach quickly vanished and it became first dazzlingly white then greyish and grained. Easily visible were the great craters gaping upside down, the ancient splashes of lighter dust that rayed out from many of them, and the vast flat plains. Visible, too, were signs of the past works of man: furrows from mining operations, fine lines that were transport networks.

By midnight the entire disk had lifted itself clear of the landscape, a satellite ceiling hanging so low it was as if one could reach up and touch it, and leaving only a narrow rim of blackness to all points of the compass. Hesper realised it was so close it must be grazing Earth's upper atmosphere. But how could this be? Long before now its approach should have heaved up such tides in sea, land and air as utterly to destroy everything upon the planet. Not only that, the satellite should be beginning to break up as a result of even greater tidal stresses induced in it by the larger body. It was a long way inside Roche's limit.

And having come this close, its trajectory should be one ending in direct collision, and that bare minutes away. Instead, this the most stunning spectacle ever beheld upon planet Earth was gliding silently and leisurely by, creating no disturbance and blithely ignoring the laws of physics. Sometime after midnight its apparent diameter began slowly to diminish, so that by dawn, when it was sliding down the opposite horizon in answer to Earth's turning, it was noticeably smaller. It was receding back into space, having given the planet a near miss.

It was, Hesper thought as the Mohists, indeed all the inhabitants of nightside Earth, stirred from their captivated vigil, just as if Earth and its moon had ceased to exert any gravitational influence on one another at all.

CHAPTER SIX

On board *ICS Standard Bearer* the command staff also watched the behaviour of Earth's moon in perplexity. Having mopped up those fugitives who had fled to the fourth planet, they had held back from pursuing the sole blip to be seen plunging into Earth's atmosphere, believing they were about to witness one of the rarest of sights: the destruction of an inhabited world through planetary collision. The business was made more eerie by the absence of the panicky exodus one might have expected; but this, Archier learned, was due to all available ships having left for Mars several days earlier.

Now the satellite was half a million miles from its onetime primary, and appeared to be following an independent orbit about the sun. Yet at its closest it had practically ploughed through Earth's atmosphere!

"Well," Archier said to his chief engineer, the only crew member he could think of who might be an expert in such matters, "is it possible?"

"What, Admiral?"

"Is it possible for gravity to cease between two orbiting bodies?"

The chief engineer, a rangy gorilla, scratched his head in puzzlement. "No sir, it isn't. When two bodies gravitate the whole weight of the universe is behind them, so to speak. I don't understand it."

"There's got to be an explanation."

"Well never mind about that now," Gruwert squealed. "Our orders are to hunt down rebels. It's safe to move in now so let's get on with it."

"First of all we shall have to reply to Earth Council."

The ships of Ten-Fleet were again beginning to gather round their flagship, a fact that had not escaped notice on Earth. For once, the presence of an Imperial fleet caused more comfort than alarm. Since Earth and the moon now shared nearly the same orbit in ignorance of one another, it would only be a matter of time before they *did* collide. Plans were already afoot to disintegrate the errant satellite or direct it into the sun. The fleet had been requested to render assistance with a planet-buster bomb.

The request had caused Archier wry amusement. It was universally assumed all Imperial fleets had magazines full of planet-busters. In fact Ten-Fleet did not have any at all. Their production had always been strictly limited and since the onset of the robot strike replacement of their degradable cores had very nearly ceased. He had heard Seventeen-Fleet still had a few in working order.

He turned to Arctus. "Tell them it would be too dangerous to disintegrate the satellite at one blow. Too many pieces would be flying around. Tell them to work out a solution using conventional FE."

A voice sounded in his ear. "*Claire de Lune* has joined formation, Admiral."

"*What?* She was supposed to have been abandoned."

"Evidently not."

"What's her report?"

"No word from her at all yet. I think her communications are out."

"Well they'll sort it out, I suppose." He was about to give the mental 'turning away' signal when his caller, the Fleet Manoeuvres Officer, continued: "Actually that isn't what I really called to tell you. The Fast Barge is approaching. We've received its blazon burst."

Archier didn't reply at once. A shiver of nervousness went through him.

"How soon?"

"Within the hour."

"All right, FMO. Thank you."

He sat brooding. Then he turned to those around him. "Did you all catch that?"

They nodded.

"It looks," he said, "as if we might finally find out what's been going on in Diadem . . ."

The Fast Barge was the property of the now defunct High Command. Consisting of little more than living quarters and a gigantic feetol drive unit, it was capable of reaching almost any part of the Empire in a remarkably short time. Ostensibly its purpose was to assist in state occasions in the outer parts of the Empire. In reality it was kept in reserve for use in an emergency, to carry messages too important or too risky to send by leader tone transmission, or as a getaway vehicle . . .

As the barge slowed down and passed the outskirts of the planetary system, its leader tone blazon announced the presence of dignitaries aboard. Minutes later Archier, in full dress uniform, waited in the reception bay with his other command officers as the barge drew alongside.

It was an impressive sight as seen on the wall screen. Nearly as big as the flagship itself, it was gridded and grilled with designs of gold and rose-pink. The shape was unusual: resembling more than anything else some over-lavishly petalled flower or orchid and owing nothing to utility.

There was a resonant *splang* as the connecting passage between the two ships sprang into place. Padding through the broad opening came a party headed by two tall and broad-shouldered men of mature years whom Archier instantly recognised: they were the Admiral Overlords Crane and Oblescu, members of the High Command Staff. But instead of dress uniform they were wearing office attire that looked stained and crumpled. Their faces were weary, even over-wrought.

An assortment of animals accompanied them: a rather scruffy enlarged mouse that scuttled alongside Crane, whiskers twitching; two dogs, a small horse and a sad-looking panda. Archier saluted smartly. Casually, the overlords responded.

"By space, but I need a pick-me-up," Crane said. "Can we go and relax somewhere? Being on that barge is like riding a roller-coaster."

"Of course, sir," Archier said stiffly. He waved back the others of his command staff and conducted the overlords to the small travelator coach that was waiting. Only the mouse—adjutant to one of the overlords, he presumed—followed them, climbing in the back of the vehicle alongside Arctus.

They zipped into the innards of the flagship, arriving at a small reception lounge Archier used for informal Force meetings. Crane and Oblescu slumped down immediately on chair-couches, while Arctus opened up the hospitality cabinet.

"What would you like, overlords?" he asked softly. "Imbibables? Smoke? Sprays or airs?"

"Give me a hash fizz," Oblescu said, "and make it good and strong."

Crane nodded in answer to Arctus' questioning trunk. The little elephant busied himself, pouring a delicate lavender fluid into three tall goblets and pressurising it with cannabis gas until it frothed.

Having quaffed and asked for more, the overlords relaxed a little. "Well, you'd better know the reason why we're here," Crane said, his tone one of tired resignation. "First of all, you know High Command doesn't really exist anymore?"

Archier nodded, toying with his goblet. "I had guessed the staff has been sent out to the fleets."

"Oh, it was only partly that. The Command was really shut down because the Imperial Council doesn't trust it any more! Things are in chaos in Diadem, the Council itself has practically collapsed. The Whole-Earth-Biotists have come to the fore again. You might as well know there's practically a civil war in the making. They're talking about bringing back the Emperor Protector. This time he's to be a Whole-Earth chimera. Genes from every permitted animal will be incorporated. If they get their way, that is."

Archier took the news with as much equanimity as he could. He had Protector sympathies himself. He was, however, far from being a Whole-Earth-Biotist. He had taken it for granted that the Protector would have one hundred per cent human genes.

"But what has this got to do with High Command?" he queried.

"Aagh." Crane gave a gesture of exasperation, which slopped fizz on his already stained uniform. "The Council ordered fleets Three and Twenty-Nine recalled so it could be sure of maintaining order. Then it came to light Seventeen and Twenty-Nine are riddled with Biotist sympathisers. Can you imagine what this did to High Command in the Council's eyes? To top it all Carusier defected to the Biotists. An Admiral Overlord! Pending a review, the Council doesn't trust Star Force at all now. It wants all the fleets kept out of Diadem, though personally I think only Seventeen and Twenty-Nine are affected."

"*Only?*" Archier echoed. "Isn't that enough?"

Arctus had stood paralysed with shock while the Admiral Overlord spoke. He turned and muttered something to the mouse, who shook his head dolefully.

"How could this happen?" Archier asked in anguish. He looked from one overlord to the other. "What went wrong?"

Oblescu jumped to his feet and paced the room. His face was distraught. "There are just too many problems! The fleets unable to handle things any longer, uprisings all over the place—Escoria hasn't been the only one! We simply don't have proper resources available any more! What with that and the lack of proper political organisation In Diadem . . . the state has been falling to pieces for some time. And now this latest disaster is one shock too many."

"Disaster? What disaster?" Archier put down his drink.

"That's the reason we are here," Crane said. "Ten-Fleet has a rather special job to do. There's something extraordinary been going on in a region some thirty light-years galactic west of here."

He paused, as if wondering how to break the news. "We have a feetol research station not far from there. We think the work it's been doing must have caused it. They weren't *trying* to get into the Simplex . . . only to advance the state of the art, stretching recession lines still farther for a faster future generation of Star Force ships. They must have gone too far. Space has opened up. There is some sort of *rent* in it, about a light year across and getting bigger. Do you grasp my meaning? The Simplex is on the other side of it! The scientists say once three-dimensional space starts to tear like that it might all come undone." He clapped a hand to his forehead. "Our universe could roll up like a scroll, as the saying is!"

While Arctus deftly and silently presented fresh drinks, Archier stared at Crane in bewilderment bordering on disbelief. "But I've never heard anything to suggest the feetol drive could damage spacetime like this," he objected.

"No, no one thought it could."

"Well what is required of me?"

"Ah. Well, the Council wants you to proceed in the direction of the rent and investigate. We didn't want to send it over the spacewaves—the whole thing has been hushed up, naturally—so I had orders to deliver the message personally. Having done that, I personally plan to retire in some out-of-the-way spot." Crane shrugged. "Of course, as you're in Condition Autonomy, you can really do what you like. In fact, as we belong to a defunct command we don't even outrank you any more!"

"I shall do what's required," Archier said slowly, "but this is a war fleet. I haven't any real scientists with me, unless there are some among the passengers."

"Yes, well I hadn't quite finished explaining. We have others working on the scientific aspects of the problem. Your role is military. I said there was nothing but the Simplex on the other side, didn't I? That isn't strictly true. There's some very strange stuff or entities or something coming through the rent, investing planets and causing chaos. We're being invaded from another facet, in other words."

"Then it's true!" Arctus trumpeted, forgetting his place. "There *are* other facets!"

"Of course," the mouse said in a measured, only slightly squeaky voice. "What else?"

"For the first time since its foundation," Oblescu put in, "the Empire faces an external rather than an internal threat. You'd think that would be enough to pull it together. Instead . . ." He trailed off.

"There's been an odd happening here too," Archier said. He explained about Earth's moon. "Do you think there's any connection?" he finished.

Crane nodded gravely. "There has to be. There isn't any other explanation. Still, I'm surprised. This is so much further away than any of the other phenomena we've heard about."

"The influence is spreading," Oblescu said.

"You call it an invasion," Archier commented, "but is it really that? What *is* taking place, exactly?"

"Information is vague. We don't think what's coming through is even matter in the way we understand it. It's not even composed of atoms. That would make sense, wouldn't it? Other facets wouldn't necessarily have the same composition as our own."

Archier brooded. "I'm at something of a loss. My previous orders also had some urgency. The Oracle says there's a weapon here in Escoria capable of destroying the Empire. Perhaps that's more important."

"Oh yes, we're supposed to tell you the Oracle has made two more pronouncements concerning the supposed 'weapon.' *It has been there a long time,* and *It has been disregarded, because it is small.* Make of it what you will. The Council wants you to give priority to the space rent thing. But as I said, since you're in Condition Autonomy—"

"I'll do as the Council says, of course," Archier said curtly. "Just as long as they are aware of what my previous orders were."

"Yes. Look, do you mind if we rest up on the flagship for a few hours? Then we'll make off on the Barge again, and find some little retreat for ourselves."

Archier was puzzled. "You're not going back to Diadem? Don't you want to do what you can to help the Empire?"

"I've already told you, we're not trusted! We've been dismissed! They wouldn't even have given us this little job if it had had any political overtones."

"I see. Well, my adjutant will take you to some staterooms."

Crane rose. He and Oblescu sauntered to the door, followed by the mouse. Before he left, Crane turned casually.

"If you make a good job of this, young feller, I dare say you'll receive promotion when a new High Command is put together. How do you fancy being an Admiral Overlord, eh?"

He laughed. But Archier could not raise a smile.

When he informed his command staff of developments, Archier was met mainly with stunned silence. Gruwert, however became excited.

" *'It has been disregarded, because it is small,' '* he repeated. "Now there's something to think on! You know what this means? The 'weapon' isn't a weapon at all! If it were a *small* weapon, it couldn't destroy an empire, that's obvious. And *'It has been there a long time'*. What are the most dangerous things, politically, sometimes lying dormant for centuries? *Ideas*, of course! What we are faced with is a political idea that's about to burst forth and give us trouble. Pre-emptive annihilation is the best way to deal with a threat like that!"

"Do you mean of all Escoria?" The image of a giraffe, relayed from *The Peaceful Star*, turned to him in Archier's conference room.

"Certainly, if we can't track it down and stamp it out any other way."

"Actually, the rumoured weapon has become a secondary consideration," Archier said, surprised by the Fire Command Officer's reaction. "Don't you think we should address ourselves first to the invasion from the Simplex?"

The pig snuffled in what sounded like annoyance. "We should take no notice of it," he said finally. "It's a natural phenomenon, like an earthquake or a star blowing. What can we do about that?"

Gruwert wasn't able to grasp the significance of it, Archier realised. Like all animals, he lacked the imagination. Only the humans present seemed really frightened.

"Perhaps, but we're going to have to forget about our task here in Escoria for the time being," he said. "The Imperial Council takes the space rent even more seriously, and therefore so shall we."

"Wait a minute!" Gruwert objected furiously. "What about apprehending rebels? There's one on Earth just waiting to be nabbed! We can't just move off and let him go free! It isn't competent!"

Archier reflected. "You're probably right. In any case, not all the fleet has reported in yet. We shan't be ready to move for several hours." He turned to Brigadier Carson of the Drop Commando. "You may make a drop. But be back in ten hours or less."

The last he heard, as he switched off the conference room, was Gruwert lustily pleading with Carson to let him accompany the mission.

CHAPTER SEVEN

To Pout, the moving city had been a disappointment. Mo, the city mind, had insisted on bombarding him with boring lectures on subjects he had no interest in. He had found the Mohists themselves irritatingly difficult to have fun with (and, mindful of the ever-watchful Mo, he had refrained from enslaving any of them with his zen gun). Also, he could feel his grip on his own little group weakening. So, calling them together (this had entailed a few electric prods-at-a-distance) he had decided to leave. Sadly he had been unable to find the girl Hesper, and if he had it would not have been much use—she was not yet under his spell.

The best thing, he told himself, was to get off this planet altogether. He toiled along now on the hills above the plain, wondering how to find a spaceport. The brothers said there was one to the south somewhere. The *kosho* would probably know—but Pout had learned already that he couldn't look to him for information. The warrior ignored all his attempts to converse.

The sun was hot, and Pout, when he glanced up and saw the glint in the sky, took it for a bird or a passing aircraft. Then, as it grew like a stone falling with terrible swiftness, he stopped while the others bunched up behind him.

The big metal shape didn't seem to slow down at all as it fell. It hit the landscape with an audible thump less than half a mile away, sending up a cloud of dust, then squatted undamaged, banging open wedge-like doors out of which poured a yelping pack of about twenty variegated figures—dogs, hyenas and cheetahs in dazzling harness and all shouting in human voices, one or two humans in bulging armour that made them look like shining robots; and, waddling to one side, encased in some sort of cloth of gold, a fat pig that sniffed and looked about him.

The carnivores all raced to and fro in intense excitement,

waiting for orders. "Oh no," quavered the eldest brother behind Pout. "Empire Commando!"

"What?" Pout knew of these much-feared shock troops, and terror struck him. But he pulled himself together. "Don't worry! You're safe with me!"

He drew the zen gun. *Kill, kill,* he thought. *Kill, kill, kill.* He was sure the gun could deal with all of them. He pressed the stud that he had learned intensified the electric stitch beam, whether to hurt, maim or kill. He pointed the muzzle and pressed the firing stud.

The wavery stitching was much weaker than he had expected. It probed towards the noisy pack, raked across the body of a dog which howled and squirmed on the ground, firing its weapons at random.

Then it went out!

Pout gaped. He pressed the intensifier stud again, squeezed the firing stud, thought of killing as hard as he could.

Nothing happened. The zen gun was not working!

Had its power pack run out? He had never even considered that it might have an exhaustible power pack. It had seemed so marvellous, so personally *his,* that he had presumed it would keep functioning as long as he kept functioning.

But now one of the armoured humans, seeing one of the dogs fall, and seeing from where the attack had come, raised an arm and pointed, bellowing a command. The whole commando unit swept forward, fanning out to form a crescent that began to sweep round Pout and his group.

He began to tremble, and his voice rose to a warbling, panicky contralto. "*Kosho!* Defend me, *kosho!* I need you!"

Ikematsu had been walking well to the rear, several paces even behind the laggard Sinbiane. When the party came to a halt he had seated himself upon the ground and entered into his customary suspended consciousness, apparently disinterested in the nearby commando landing.

At Pout's summons he rose, turning slowly to survey the scene. A few strides took him in advance of Pout's frightened following and there he stood, still in seeming trance, his eyes half closed, his face expressionless.

An astonishing transformation came over his accoutrements. He did not move his hands or raise his arms from his sides. But the rifles he carried in his rack rose of their own volition, hovering around his head and shoulders. Partly they were under his mental control, partly extensions of his nervous system and knowing themselves what they should do. Selectively, they let loose a barrage of fire. At his waist, his mortar tube began to lob grenades, picking out patches of ground in flashes of green fire.

The commandos opened fire too. The hovering rifles darted this way and that. Every beam and missile, despatched from a variety of weapons, aimed at Pout's party was intercepted by the defensive umbrella the *kosho* projected.

Suddenly there was silence. Ikematsu had killed cheetahs; he had killed dogs; he had killed hyenas. He had not killed either of the two humans or the pig; these were high-ranking personages, and they gave the order now for the surviving commandos to withdraw. They were amazed; they had never before seen a rifle that could cancel out the energy beam from another rifle.

Gruwert had scuttled back into the drop pod. He peered round the edge of the door. "Who's that?" he demanded angrily. "We're fighting a single man?"

"It looks like a *kosho*," Brigadier Carson told him. He still stood on the ground, but had retreated to where it was only a step to safety. "An ancient mystical warrior order. They're only found on Earth. I'd heard they were pretty remarkable, but this . . ."

"*What?* Why didn't anyone tell me? *They* might be the weapon!"

"I don't think so. They are forbidden to take sides in power politics."

Ruefully Carson surveyed the scene before the pod. He had lost about half his animals. The survivors, having withdrawn to the shadow of the pod, stood tense, noses pointed to the *kosho*. A word from him or Major Kastrillo, the only other human in the party, and they would bound into action again totally disregardful of their own lives.

He had no intention, however, of expending them needlessly. He was about to order them back into the pod with a view to bombing the Earthites from the air when the *kosho* came striding towards him. The commando animals growled; he could see them focusing their skullguns. Unperturbed, the *kosho* stopped a few yards away.

"My principal would request a cessation of hostilities," he said calmly. "We have no interest in each other."

"You killed my animals," Carson retorted hotly.

"You attacked us."

"You attacked first."

"True," the *kosho* replied equably. "My principal was perturbed at your behaviour, which he believed presaged an assault upon us. That, too, is my impression."

"What is all this talk?" Gruwert squealed quietly to Carson. "Scan him to dust—No, wait!"

A new thought had struck the pig. Cautiously he descended to the ground. "How would you like to have such fighters in your commando, Brigadier?" he murmured. "These fellows could prove mighty useful."

"But the cooperation of a *kosho* is almost impossible to acquire," Carson reminded him.

"Oh really? But he isn't a free agent as it is. You just heard him say he's acting under orders." Gruwert spoke up and addressed the warrior. "Who is this principal of yours? Point him out to me."

"He is the manlike chimera who first fired on you."

"Bring him here," Gruwert said, peering in Pout's direction. "We want to talk to him."

"Under safe conduct?"

Major Carson nodded.

Ikematsu walked back to Pout. "Listen carefully," he said. "I have defended your life and my obligation to you is over. But I will perform you one more service, for a price.

"These are fighters from Diadem, the centre of the Empire. You would like to leave Earth and go to Diadem, would you not? Yes, I know you would. Above our heads is a huge fleet with thousands of men and animals on board. Eventually it will go to Diadem. I will talk to the officers from the fleet. I will persuade them that they should take you with them.

"All I want in return is that gun you have."

"This gun?" Hopefully Pout tendered the scangun he had taken from Hesper Positana.

"No, the other gun."

Pout's ears twitched and his eyes widened pitifully. The *kosho* had approached the strangers without a word to him, leaving him bewildered and frightened. He gazed down at the dead gun in his other hand, then clutched it to his chest.

"No!" he mewled. "My beautiful gun! I won't give up my gun!"

"It does not even work any more."

"It *will* work!" Pout spat desperately. "One day it will work!"

"Had I a mind I could kill you here, for the harm and the hatred in you, and take the gun."

These words frightened Pout and he dodged aside from Ikematsu to run towards the armoured men and the animals standing by the big metal thing. He was less afraid of them, at this moment, than he was of his onetime protector.

Balefully the predators glared at him, but he ignored them and fell to his knees before the two humans. "I am a nice animal!" he gasped. "I love the Empire! Save me from those people!"

A cheery voice came suddenly from inside the pod. "Now, now, what's all this panic?"

The men moved apart. Pout found himself staring into a fat-jowled pig face with twinkling little eyes. "Things are getting confusing," Gruwert remarked. "Tell me, is it not you who is supposed to be the, er, *master* of that *kosho* over there?"

"Yes, yes, I am," babbled Pout.

"Now there's an odd thing in itself. He looks pure human to me, and you . . . well, what *are* you exactly?"

A hint of pride came into Pout's voice. "I am a chimera of every primate species, sir." He spoke respectfully, realizing he was in the presence of authority. Indeed, something about the pig's manner reminded him of the role of Torth Nascimento in the museum . . .

Gruwert waddled from the pod once more. He raised his snout and sniffed the air with a loud snuffling sound. "Really? Now that *is* interesting. They say this is the planet we all came from. The old Earth herself, cradle of our *biota*. Just the place, one might think, to find something *unusual*, shall we say? Well, citizen—you *are* a citizen, aren't you? Of course you are: a citizen of the second class, like myself. Now citizen, we didn't mean you any harm. We spotted your group from up in space and decided to talk to you, that's basically it. It seems we gave you a fright—our commandos *are* a bit rough, I admit! But you see, there has been much wickedness in this sector and it's our business to deal with it. You wouldn't believe it, but there are criminals in Escoria who are against the Empire and want to plunge us all back into barbarism. We are looking for one who landed in this region a few days ago. It's very bare country hereabouts, so maybe you can help us?" Gruwert's tone hardened. "Where is he?"

"It isn't a he, it's a girl!" Pout offered eagerly. "She wore a black and silver suit and came down in an egg! Look, she gave me this scangun."

Gruwert watched while Major Kastrillo took the weapon from Pout's grasp, glanced at it, then tossed it through the door of the drop pod. "Yes, that's the one," he said slowly. The rebels tracked to Mars had worn the same uniform. "Let's have her, then."

"Oh, she's not here, she's—"

Pout stopped. He wondered how much bargaining power his knowledge of the girl's whereabouts gave him—and did he dare try to use it?

He glanced back. The *kosho* and his young nephew were walking slowly towards him!

His skin prickled. "I am glad to be of service to the Empire," he said obsequiously. Then, in a voice of panic: "Take me with you and I'll tell you where she is!"

"You are coming with us anyway," Gruwert said commandingly. "Now quickly, end this deviousness."

While Ikematsu and Sinbiane stood silently by, Pout said: "There are some moving cities that roam flat ground over that way." He waved an arm. "She's in the nearest of them. It's called Mo."

"Yes, we saw them. *Where* in this city?"

Pout shrugged. "They're not as large as all that."

"I suppose that will do," Gruwert said, satisfied. "All right, get inside the pod."

"Are you really taking the chimera?" Brigadier Carson asked in surprise.

"Yes, I am." Gruwert had dark thoughts about the creature. Though he had spoken to him as though to a child, he suspected there might be considerably more to him than that. Why was the *kosho*, a proud and highly trained human being—he recalled something about *koshos* now—apparently his servant? A pan-primate chimera, too . . . it was reminiscent of the pan-mammalian chimera the Whole-Earth-Biotists wanted to install as Emperor Protector.

"We'll take the *kosho* too," he decided. "Don't they have special mental training? Heightened psychic flexibility?" He pondered. It was, he supposed, exactly the faculty—heightened imagination—which animals were supposed to be incapable of. "That's the sort of quality we might need if we're to investigate that rent in space."

"Yes, you're absolutely right," muttered Carson. Yet looking at the imperturbable warrior, and his array of weapons, he wondered exactly how he was to be 'taken'.

Pout was stopped from entering the pod by a dog who came up to him and began sniffing him all over. The beast stood nearly as tall as Pout himself; the chimera cringed but the commando persisted, and eventually its muzzle lunged and came out gripping the zen gun he had put back in his bib.

"He had another gun," the dog growled between clenched teeth.

"It doesn't work. It's my lucky charm." Pout watched with pleading eyes as Carson took the gun and turned it over. The man grunted in amusement, then pointed it at the horizon and squeezed the trigger. Nothing happened.

"It's made of wood," he remarked lightly. "Only an old curio." Pout timorously extended a paw; he casually handed the gun back to him.

On seeing Pout skulk his way into the pod, tucking the gun in his bib, Ikematsu stepped forward. "If I am to come with you I must keep my weapons," he said to the Brigadier. "A *kosho* does not discard his armoury."

Indignantly Carson looked at him. "We're not allowing you on one of our ships rigged out like that! You're a walking war!" He waved Sinbiane back. "And we don't need you, young man. You stay here."

"This is my nephew," Ikematsu informed. "I go nowhere without him."

Suddenly he made a series of quick movements, disengaging the catches of his harness, at which the rifle rack, the mortar tube and the other weapons fell away, arranging themselves on the ground with surprising neatness.

"See," he said, "I disarm, contrary to all principle, provided my nephew accompanies me. I ask only that my armoury be stored safely and returned to me eventually."

"Oh, all right," Carson agreed. He was relieved that the *kosho* was being cooperative, not guessing that Ikematsu's first demand had been no more than a bargaining counter.

He and the major helped the animals drag their dead into the pod for space burial later. Squatting inside the pod, the cheetahs especially cast feral glances at the *kosho;* but their discipline restrained them from any threatening word or gesture.

The pod lifted off. In the orbiting cruiser they delayed only while the bodies and the prisoners were transferred. Then they dropped, with the other pods Carson ordered, onto Mo.

Five hundred commandos sliced through the moving city with a ferocity its inhabitants could hardly have envisaged. Even so, it was nearly four hours before the fugitive had been located and taken prisoner.

That gave time for the pig Fire Command Officer to learn about the life style of the cities of the plain. He was reminded once again of his conclusions concerning the Oracle's pronouncements; accordingly, he engineered another small, but personal, triumph. With referring to Admiral Archier, he called his own department and arranged to have the whole plain nuked as they departed.

"Those cities are a social experiment," he explained to Brigadier Carson as they watched the pinpricks of light blossom on the curve of the planet below them. "An experiment in academics: they spend—spent, rather—their whole time studying—studying *history* and *social philosophy*, among other things. Can't be too careful. No knowing what ideas they were brewing. Could be what the Oracle was talking about."

Carson had misgivings. "The Admiral will be annoyed if he hears about it. He's supposed to give the order for things like that."

"Oh, don't worry," Gruwert said jovially. "He can't attend to every little detail, can he?"

And some of you humans, the pig added to himself with satisfaction, aren't so hot when it comes to making decisions.

In *Claire de Lune*'s command centre Ragshok had synched into the Fleet Manoeuvres Network. On the screens he saw the current dispositions as the last few ships—of a rather depleted fleet since the battle with the Escorians, he noticed—joined formation. He had learned to read some of the codes, too. He had identified, for instance, the code for what he now thought of as his own ship, and had been able to respond to instructions.

Although it was only hours since he had joined the fleet, so far there had been no trouble. He had ignored beamed requests for reports, and as far as he knew no one had tried to come through the intermat, though as it wasn't working yet it was hard to be sure. Probably they would despatch someone in a boat sooner or later. Things could get tricky.

He called Tengu again. "Well?"

The image of the systems engineer appeared in the air before him. "Not yet. I'm still checking. If there's a fault, I'll find it, I swear."

But Tengu looked worried, and Ragshok cursed. After all their work, this had to happen!

Installing the flux unit from his ship *Dare* had been no small job for a start. While that was under way he had toured half a dozen worlds, picking up rebel fugitives who had managed to evade pursuit following the battle, privateer gangs like his own, and anyone he could persuade to throw in with him and who could use a weapon.

He had packed nearly three thousand men and women into *Claire de Lune*. They would be getting restless if he didn't soon produce what he had promised them.

His whole plan depended on getting the intermat working. Tengu had earlier inspected the transceiver kiosks and announced them undamaged, despite not properly understanding how they functioned. The fact that they would not work within the bounds of the ship had seemed reasonable at the time: they were a ship-to-ship facility, and he had presumed there would be no problems once they came within range of the rest of the fleet.

But how long would the Imperial staff remain incurious about a ship that was supposed to have been abandoned?

"Speed it up, will you," he grated to Tengu, dismissing him.

"Eh chief," said Morgan, messing about at the comdesk. "Look at this."

Ragshok squinted at the display area as Morgan put up the data Fleet Manoeuvres was putting out. "It's a general order," Morgan said. "They're moving out."

"Where to?"

Morgan shook his head. "Just somewhere. Nowhere interesting. To the next bit of trouble, I guess."

"Damn Tengu!" raged Ragshok. "This is his fault! I trusted him!"

"What shall we do?"

"You can get the GDC and everything out of that?"

He was referring to Galactic Directional Coordinates. "Yes, I think so," Morgan said.

"Then we obey orders."

Tentatively, for he still was not too expert at handling the

Planet Class destroyer, Morgan entered figures on his desk, called the engine room, and began to manoeuvre.

Somehow or other he got into formation. The fleet withdrew from the system, meshing bubbles, and hurtled for the unknown.

CHAPTER EIGHT

Diadem—Galactic Diadem, or the Jewel in the Galactic Crown, as it was variously known in official documents— presented to the approaching visitor a splendid sight of depth within depth, of stars of every size and colour grouped, constellated, strewn and focused in patterns of dazzling complexity that no jeweller could ever have equalled. Perhaps even more exciting, to one from the outer parts of the Empire, was the thought of the splendours, invisible from his first vantage point, of the inhabited planets Diadem contained. In the past the development of the Diadem worlds had been on a colossal scale. There were cities which, like the starry perspective of Diadem itself, exhibited depth upon depth of architectural glory, though many of these were inhabited mainly by animals now, and there were worlds galore with sculpted climates and reconstituted biospheres that rendered them planetary paradises, each according to the private tastes of its owner, though maintenance had been cursory in the decades of the robot strike and on some of them nature had already begun to take its own course.

How it appeared to the large vessel that entered, with the permission of the Imperial Council (Diadem being one of the few regions of the galaxy where absolute territorial rights between alien races were respected), and leisurely made its way to a slightly bluish sun, was a different matter. The Methorians did not see in the comparatively short wavelengths that composed the visible spectrum for humans, and in fact did not see sharply defined solid objects at all. On their own planets were no standing cities, no fixed structures but instead gauzy rolling masses that floated and circulated within the atmospheric bands characteristic of gas giants.

Imperial Council Member Koutroubis arrived at the fifth planet of the sun only a short time ahead of the scheduled meeting with the Methorian delegate, an event he did not look forward to in the least. The planet, a light-year from the group of worlds where the Council was accustomed to sitting, was a private residence that had been chosen mainly for its placid traffic-free atmosphere, but also because it was the home of an old friend of his who was always willing to do a favour.

Oskay Rubadaya, a white-haired man of middling years, waved his arms in greeting as Koutroubis's official statecar descended to land just outside one of the many lodges he had dotted about the planet. The lodge itself was a rambling construction extending for about a mile in any direction. Before it there stretched a level meadow of pale green moss reaching almost to the horizon—the reason why the site had been selected. On its fringes arboreal parkland began. It was Rubadaya's pleasure to go for long walks through that parkland, a recurring feature over the whole planet. He was particularly fond of trees; the parks had been planned and planted by a tax-item artist from one of the outer regions of the Empire.

Koutroubis stepped down from the statecar. "Hello Oskay." He sniffed the air. "Why, how . . . er, *odd* the atmosphere seems."

"*Innocent* is the word you're looking for," Rubadaya chuckled. "What's unusual is that there's nothing artificial in the atmosphere. No perfumes or psychotropics. Mostly what you're smelling is tree resins."

"Mm, I see." Koutroubis glanced anxiously at the sky. "I'm a little early."

"Then come and get some refreshment." Rubadaya led the way through the entrance to the lodge and into a spacious timbered room. He called out several times, until eventually a household robot sauntered casually in.

"Um, this is the Council Member I told you about, Hoskiss. I was wondering if you would be good enough to mix us some drinks. This *is* a special guest."

A sighing noise came from the robot's speaker. "Of course, sir," it said, in a tone conveying something other than servility. With perfunctory correctness it moved to a cabinet, busied itself with squirts and gushes, and served tall glasses on a tray.

"Thank you, Hoskiss!" Rubadaya said fulsomely. "I really am grateful."

"I hope so, sir. Now if you'll excuse me, I'm going to sun myself on the patio for the rest of the day."

The robot left. "Well at least you can get him to do *something* for you," Koutroubis smiled.

The robot union gave household robots total discretion as to how or whether they served their masters. Rubadaya shook his head in exasperation. "He does just as he likes," he said. "You know, we have to pay them more respect than if they *were* recognised as sentients. At least as second-class citizens they'd have to do what they were told! Why don't we give them what they want?"

"Please!" Koutroubis groaned, putting his hand to his forehead. "No more problems now! We've got enough as it is!"

"Just as you please." Rubadaya, like most humans in Diadem, lived virtually oblivious of political matters. He was one of those who took the Empire for granted but didn't even seem to care if it was maintained or not. Sometimes Koutroubis wondered if he should resent such profound disinterest, but there was no way round it. One couldn't have a free society and coerce people as well—not, at any rate, the most privileged and civilised members of that society, which in this case meant the first-class citizenry of Diadem.

He sucked his drink through the straw provided. "What's the population of this planet?" he asked conversationally.

"There are three of us. Fuong, who spends most of his time on an island chain on the big ocean—that's just about diametrically opposite us here—and an old lady who's built herself a town on the equator. She has a few animals with her. It does feel a bit crowded sometimes. Always seem to be bumping into one or the other of them, though I suppose a bit of company is welcome occasionally." Rubadaya shrugged. "As I'm the freeholder I could ask them to find planets of their own, but it wouldn't be neighbourly, I feel."

He laid down his glass. "I'm curious about this meeting. It sounds so awkward. Couldn't messengers be used instead, or something?"

"I'm afraid not," Koutroubis said with a deep sigh. Methorians had a gaseous metabolism instead of the liquid one evolved in water oceans. The structure corresponding to the basic cell was a balloon-like gasbag. And communication was accomplished by means of gaseous diffusion of coded molecules. "When Methorians parley," he explained, "they engulf one another in a mutal gaseous effusion. There has to be personal proximity, or nothing significant has happened.

They insist on the same in their rare dealings with us. Apparently they feel psychologically that we haven't taken any notice of them, otherwise."

"What kind of 'gaseous effusion' are you going to give off?" Rubadaya asked with amusement.

"That's all arranged."

"Why does it have to be *us* who accommodate *them?*" Rubadaya rubbed his chin thoughtfully. "Isn't their technology more advanced than ours? You'd think gaseous creatures, especially being as huge and fragile as they are, would find it pretty difficult to be space travellers at all."

"Yes, they are pretty big, and unwieldy, as you say. But I wouldn't say their technology's any better than ours overall. Perhaps not as good. They are a much older race than we are, but everything's taken them much longer. For their first few million years they had no proper concept of a solid object, for instance.

"Actually they use a trick for space travel; they compress themselves. It's possible for a gas creature, you know. It's uncomfortable, I believe, but without it their ships would have to be simply enormous. They're ten times the size of ours as it is."

A voice sounding in his ear sent Koutroubis's nervous apprehension leaping up the scale. It was his spider monkey pilot.

"They're coming in, sir."

"Let's watch the thing land," Koutroubis suggested to Rubadaya as he came to his feet. "Ought to be quite a sight."

Outside, they could see a small ball high in the sky. It was the Methorian landing craft. Having detached itself from the main ship outside the atmosphere, it was inflating as it descended, allowing its occupant to decompress and assume full size.

By the time it came to sink close to the meadow the ball was a rippling sphere about a hundred feet in diameter. Gently it settled, its underbelly swelling on the moss, putting out tendrils which gripped the turf and steadied it.

"Wish me luck," Koutroubis said glumly.

His staff of primates and elephants hurried towards him with the atmosuit and gas generator trolley he would need inside the sphere. He allowed them to garb him and lead him forward to the orifice that plopped open in the bulging skin. It was like entering a pale orange mouth, which closed behind him. Then the throat opened, and he moved forward into a reddish medium he knew to be composed of hydrogen, methane, ammonia and countless complex volatiles.

Visually, it was confusing. The gases of the globe's interior swayed and swirled, mainly, it seemed, because of the constantly windmilling motion of the Methorian, which occupied about a third of the available space. It was hard to make out the creature clearly; more than anything else it reminded Koutroubis of a gigantic multihued jellyfish suspended in the murky air, the central mass surrounded by wavy translucent veils tipped with filaments. Gas-giant life was, he had been told, of such delicacy that a human being could not come into physical contact with it without doing it some damage.

The trolley had obediently followed him into the sphere and now began serving its function of expelling code gases that soughed out and mingled with the atmosphere. He had been assured these would give the Methorian the needed psychological experience of a *communicating presence* that at the same time carried a sufficiently individual tang to give it the tag of being alien and human.

The job of language translation had fortunately been handled by the Methorians. A low but melodiously clear voice spoke to him, emanating from nowhere in particular.

"I am the delegate that was sent."

"I welcome you to Diadem, centre of our Empire," Koutroubis responded.

"Normally such visits are not needed. Our races live in different environments, supplying neither common interest nor points of conflict. We do, however, inhabit the same spacetime. A rupture has appeared in the meshwork that composes this spacetime. Through this rupture our instruments discern the Simplex; the veil of the world is torn, exposing the lacework."

Koutroubis swallowed. He knew full well the accusation that was coming. The Methorian was probably using metaphors appropriate to his own lifeform. A human would have said 'face' and 'bones' rather than 'veil' and 'lacework.'

"What can it mean?" the creature continued. "Through the tear come incomprehensibles that cause havoc on three of our worlds. We ask ourselves what our scientists or engineers have done to create this catastrophe. We find nothing. We ask the other races with which we share the galaxy. From Diadem comes a positive answer. I must now ask you to confirm that answer in person.''

Had it been given a proper opportunity, the Imperial Council might well have preferred to dissemble about the matter. Unluckily a reply had been transmitted direct, in between Council meetings, by a group of tax-item scientists working in the civil service. It was too late to back out now.

''Yes,'' Koutroubis said wearily, ''we think—only *think*, mind—that one of our research facilities might have been responsible. It was working on feetol technique—the same that your ships use.''

''What is to be done? The rent grows bigger. Sentient beings in *all* galaxies might soon have cause to criticise your behaviour. I am instructed to ask what remedial action is proposed.''

''We're working on it,'' Koutroubis said doggedly.

''May I receive relevant technical information? We too will seek a way to avert catastrophe, the case being possibly dire.''

''Yes, I think I can arrange that.''

I *hope* I can arrange it, Koutroubis corrected himself. Even the civil service was now in disarray. The Council had lost much of its power of action.

By the Simplex, he wasn't even sure if the emergency science team *had* been assembled in the end!

But it wouldn't do to try to explain such confusion to the Methorian.

CHAPTER NINE

For the hundredth time Tengu finished checking the circuitry of the intermat kiosk and put his logic probe back in his pocket, his face displaying a now-familiar feeling of aggravation mixed with anxiety. There was nothing wrong either with the switching or with the feetol interface that enwrapped the cubicle and on which the system depended. Of course, he didn't really know how the intermat worked, and there was one new introduction into the ship's workings as a whole—the replacement flux unit. It delivered a flux curve that was perfectly normal—but could the old ruined one have added some necessary kink, perhaps? If so he would never find out what it was.

But he didn't dare tell Ragshok that. Ragshok's rages could be terrible.

After closing the panel, and as a matter of routine procedure, he tapped out the flagship code from the list beside the touch buttons, and fatalistically pressed *GO*.

For a blinding instant white light filled the kiosk. He blinked, then realized he was no longer in the same kiosk. The location plate had changed from *Claire de Lune* to *Standard Bearer*.

Tengu's heart went into his mouth. For what reason he could not fathom, it had worked! He was on board the flagship!

Cautiously he pushed open the door. He was acquainted with the luxurious interior of the *Claire de Lune*, and he had heard of the extravagance of Diadem.

But the sight that met his eyes was far beyond anything he would have anticipated in a ship of war.

Archier took the slight, florid figure who crept from the kiosk and peered down into the salon for a crewman who had sneaked to the ball while on shift. What made him noticeable was that he wore no costume, only a ragged shirt that flapped over stained breeks and was cinched at the waist by a tool belt. No doubt he felt out of place and he deserved a reprimand, but Archier let it go.

He had permitted the victory ball to go ahead despite the seriousness of what lay ahead. The theme of the ball was Nemesis. Like most others, he wore a costume of electrically stiffened fabric that in its unexcited state was gauzy, limp and colourless, but which in answer to the currents flowing from a little generator mat could be pulled and shaped, could be given any variety of hues, translucencies and textures. The human figures that pranced the floor of the salon were an average of twelve foot in height, representing ancient gods of war, glowing warships and weapons of total destruction, giant masks of dread, aggressive abstract shapes. Animals were similarly bedecked, but in a manner adapted to their forms; long shapes worn by the four-footed darted about the ballroom, sometimes fronted with slavering jaws and sometimes play-fully crashing into one another.

To the watcher on the mezzanine where the intermat kiosks were placed the pulsing streamers of light that bedecked the salon would also seemed to be joined by a dreadful cacophony; about a dozen kinds of music were punishing the air at once. The costumed dancers, however, carried sound filters; they could tune in to the airs of their taste.

"It's *sick*, Admiral! It's all completely *sick!*"

The girlish voice belonged to Hesper Positana, the last of the rebels to be captured. He turned and at first thought that in her silver and black uniform she was entering into the spirit of the thing. But her sulky face told otherwise.

She had been railing at Archier at every opportunity since being introduced to him. She should have been on the vessel that had been designated as a prison ship, but having been brought aboard together with the three Earthites, she had been left where she was.

Archier's painted face smiled at her through the folds of Indra's cummerbund. "But fun, you'll agree."

"*Fun?*" Hesper gaped at him in outrage. "Admiral, I hardly think *fun* is the word that should be used when describing the behaviour of imperialists. What have you got here? A celebration of oppression and random violence! Maybe that's fun for you, but as far as I'm concerned it's merely vile."

"I assure you we don't see ourselves that way."

"So how do you see the nuke bombs you dropped on Earth, for instance? What need was there for that?"

Archier shook his head, setting the baleful face of Indra swaying. "But no such thing happened."

"Don't kid me. I saw the fireballs after we took off."

Leaning closer so he could make himself heard over the music, Archier said, "You're placing the blame in the wrong quarter. An insurgent can't claim to be on the side of peace. What safety can there be without Imperial stability? It's my duty to maintain it."

"Huh! The Empire!" Disdainfully Hesper waved at the scene before her. "Just look at it! A pack of degenerates and perverts! Wallowing with animals, with cattle and wild beasts! It's pathetic!"

"Yes, I know that intelligent animals aren't allowed into decent society on many of the outer worlds. But is that attitude creditable, or even civilised? All mammals are part of the same family. And the Empire does need their services."

"We don't need them in Escoria, not at all. And do you know why, Admiral? Because we have lots of real *people*, and that's because we *breed*. We have lots of *children*, remember them? Why don't you try it? Family life's not so bad."

She took a deep breath. "But it's not surprising you've forgotten what sex is for when one takes a look at your women, is it? Why are they so *hideous?* Why would anyone want to make herself look so *old?*"

Archier smiled again to see how hopelessly provincial Hesper's outlook was. She had absolutely no comprehension of current fashionable ides of female beauty.

And now one of the aged faces she despised so much called out to him from within the pulsating flanges of a flashblast projector costume.

"Admiral! Come and dance with me!"

As he swept into the melee, Archier saw a look of jealous puzzlement fleetingly across Hesper's face.

Not far away Gruwert, his costume switched off, the fabric hanging like rags about his corpulent bristly form, talked earnestly to Pout the chimera.

"So how do you *gain* your followers?" he asked.

For answer Pout smiled idiotically, his large eyes swivelling mysteriously towards the ceiling.

Gruwert gave an exasperated snuffle. He knew that this amalgam of primates could not be as stupid as he acted. Not to have all those people in tow, most of them apparently much brighter than himself.

These apes always were a shifty lot, he told himself. And that went for the hairless variety, too.

And in a corridor some yards from the room where Gruwert was entertaining Pout, Hako Ikematsu sat cross-legged in the rest position, inasmuch as a *kosho* could ever be said to rest. His spine was erect, his arms spread in the prescribed position, but his consciousness was not in suspension. He had merely blanked out his thoughts to make himself receptive to the emanations of others.

That way he was able to keep track of the presence of the man-ape chimera. Pout's mental signature was distinctive: crafty, greedy thoughts in a brew of resentful malevolence that was, Ikematsu recognised, merely the perversion of the love of life that was natural to all mammals, but which in this case had been much ill-used.

Alongside it he sensed another presence, another signature: a sort of thrusting, porcine forcefulness, an impression of rooting, trampling power.

It was the tang of empire.

Chaotic music from the ballroom drifted up the corridor as a door opened at the far end, then was cut off again. Sinbiane and his new friend, a dark-eyed boy of about the same age whose black hair was gathered behind his head in a knot, approached.

"Hello uncle. This is Trixa. He's on the battle staff here. He works the big guns. I told him you were a great warrior on Earth."

Ikematsu rose to his feet and smiled down at the boy. "So you fought in the battle they are celebrating?"

"Yes sir," Trixa told him boldly. "I coordinate eight guns here on the flagship. I helped knock out four of the enemy." He paused. "Have you killed many people, sir?"

Ikematsu continued smiling. "I have killed no one, young cannoneer."

" 'A true warrior does not kill by his own hand,' " Sinbiane intoned to the puzzled boy, " 'but only by the unavoidable fate of he who is killed.' "

"Fate?" echoed Trixa. "But there isn't any such thing!"

* * *

Sweating, Tengu found Ragshok in *Claire de Lune*'s restaurant. He was talking to Morgan and the Salpian engineer, Drue.

"The intermat," Tengu choked out. "It's started working!"

Ragshok's eyes lit up. He licked his lips.

The Salpian had been eating from a plate in rapid gulps. He pushed it away. "It figures! I should have guessed it!"

Tengu stared at him.

"I was just telling the chief what I found out," the engineer explained. "Whenever this fleet flies in feetol formation, all the bubbles merge into one big bubble. That's why Imperial fleets are faster than our own ships. For the intermat to work, you must have to be inside the big bubble too."

"These Imperials got a lot of tricks up their sleeve," Morgan said admiringly.

"Let's see them trick their way out of this one." Ragshok leaned towards Tengu. "Are you sure it's working? Have you been through?"

"Sure. To the flagship and back. I spent half an hour there."

He would have stayed longer, once the smokes in the air got to him. But he had become nervous because of the looks he was getting. Besides, he had wanted to make sure he could get back.

"The flagship, no less," Ragshok murmured. "What did you find there?"

"It's weird. There's some sort of victory dance going on. They call this a warfleet? It's more like a ride down the Janja." He was referring to a famous river replete with pleasure boats.

"A celebration. What a time to strike! And anyway, we have to do it before the fleet comes out of feetol. Did you see many arms about?"

"Nobody was armed that I could see. It looks easier than taking a passenger liner, by far."

"Okay. It will take an hour or more to get ready to move. Choose some men and reconnoitre the bigger ships, if you can do it discreetly. Make sure it's the same all over."

Broodingly Ragshok stared down into the main area of the restaurant from the executive's balcony he had reserved for himself. They had got the dispenser operating and now everybody came to the restaurant for meals. Like the ship, it was overcrowded, and noisy too. In at least three places brawls were going on.

"We're going to do it," he said in a dreamlike voice. "We're going to seize an Imperial Star Force fleet, one of the greatest instruments of power the galaxy has seen."

"And then we're going to rape Diadem," Morgan finished for him.

"That's right. The greatest act of pillage in history. It will be just like taking some ripe, defenceless woman—Diadem doesn't have any defences of its own. There are only the Star Force fleets, and they are out in the Empire."

"They could soon be recalled," Drue pointed out.

"Too late. It will be a stand-off: we give them the message, move in and we start blasting worlds."

"And if they promise the same for Escoria?" Tengu asked softly.

Ragshok's answer was a ferocious growl. "We let them! What's it to us? The Empire will fall to pieces and we pick up Diadem as first prize."

He stood up, pointing to Tengu. "You and Morgan see to the reconnoitre. I'll round up our tem leaders and organise the squads."

Just then an odd, transient event took place. In the air before him Ragshok seemed to see fine silvery threads, straight as tracks of light and sparkling from end of the restaurant to the other. It was like a linear cobweb being spun just too fast for the eye to catch. But in a second or two the apparition was gone.

"What in the Simplex was *that?*" he demanded.

When, in the ballroom aboard *Standard Bearer*, Archier noticed similar threads, this time glinting obliquely from floor to ceiling, he took them for an arranged visual effect, a presage to some extravagance to come. Then word was brought to him. Something unexplained was happening.

He summoned Arctus and made his way to the Command Centre. On the way there they saw the threads again. This time they started at the farther end of the corridor and proceeded at moderate pace down it, looking, he thought, like an array of lines marking the interfaces of metallic crystals. But, before they reached him, they vanished.

In the Command centre he found the white-haired Menshek and a number of ship engineers, including the chief engineer he had questioned earlier over the behaviour of Earth's moon. Menshek was talking earnestly with the duty officer, a young tiger.

With a spasm of guilt at having such a thought, Archier suddenly found himself wishing some of the engineers could have been human. Animals weren't at their best when handling the totally unknown.

"These lines that are appearing in the air," Menshek said to him. "We're getting the same reports from all over the fleet. In fact we think they're appearing over a wide region of space. It must be another manifestation from the rent."

"The instruments showed a very brief interruption in the operation of the engines," the gorilla chief engineer told him. "That could be serious. But it hasn't recurred yet."

"We're not supposed to be in the affected region yet," Archier remarked.

"It's probably spread."

"Are we close to any stars?"

"Yes sir," the duty officer informed him gruffly. "We are about to sidestep a system with an inhabited planet, as a matter of fact. We'll pass within three light-days."

"We'd best make for it. Our investigation can start there. Decelerate and alter course."

While the tiger obeyed, quietly speaking instructions, the cobweb lines reappeared. Archier could see now that they emerged from the walls. They gave him the impression of being immensely, immensely long—light-years, at least.

They vanished. "What do you make of it?" Archier asked Menshek. He paused. "Could they be something to do with recession lines?"

"Nothing in our universe could make recession lines visible," Menshek pointed out. "But did you ever watch Cursom's book on what other facets might be like? Purely speculative, of course, but the point is they might not consist of three-dimensional realms containing particulate matter, like ours. The 'flattening' or collapse of the Simplex might take other forms, well-nigh incomprehensible to our intellects. Specifically, Cursom predicts there will be facets where it's the recession lines, not the particles they connect, that become the 'material entities', while the original particles would play the part of separating locations or end-points. The fundamental unit of such a facet would not be a pointlike particle but a sort of extensible line, no limit being placed on length. Such lines, infinitesimal in themselves, would be able to collect themselves together to form the equivalent of higher structures—atoms, molecules and so forth—but always strictly in parallel. The threads we have seen answer to that description. They might even be living forms.''

"Linear matter," Archier pondered, while the animals stared, struggling to comprehend. "But could it exist in our kind of space?''

"Perhaps, once it arrived here. Or perhaps their space and ours is intermingling.''

"And if they are intelligent, how would *they* see *us?*''

"Ah, that's a question.'' Menshek seemed to find the question intriguing. Briefly he turned to watch the data form in the air as the Fleet Manoeuvres Department did its work. "They would lack our sense of individuality as something existing at a defined place—indeed, they would scarcely understand the notion of 'place' as we do. Their equivalent of a single particle might sometimes extend throughout the whole of their spacetime, and it would be the same for larger structures. For them, the concept of 'being' would be associated with linear dispersal.

"They might not, yet, have been able to find anything here they can recognise as having material properties.''

Archier sighed fretfully. "I wish Diadem could have sent us a scientist! We're out of our depth!''

"Have you tried to find any among the passengers?'' Menshek asked. 'Passengers' was how Star Force crews referred to the inevitable hangers-on aboard ships of the fleets.

"I did put the word out, but you know how reluctant these people are to get involved in anything.''

"Perhaps you should have made it clear what's involved.''

Archier shook his head. "There's state security to think of.''

The conversation was interrupted by a sound of tumult from outside. Snarling softly, the duty officer whirled round as though the door there burst a shouting group of what Archier, because they still wore costume, the bellicose images rearing above those who were human, presumed at first were revellers who had inconsiderately intruded into the working area.

But they were clearly terrified. A lissom-figured young woman, her senile face set into the belly of a writhing, evil-looking Mother Kali, rushed up to him, her woe-begone expression an incongruous contrast.

"Admiral!" she screamed. "They're coming through the intermats! They're killing everybody!"

Archier tried to free himself of the clutching arms of both herself and her costume.

"Who?"

"Rebels! Pirates! I don't know!"

Shucking off its silvery-grey covering that vaguely resembled a feetol shell, an impala trotted up to Archier to paw him nervously. "Savages, Admiral, savages! Do you know what they're wearing? *Animal skins!* Do you hear me? *Animal skins!*"

The impala's voice broke on a hysterical note.

"Call commando quarters," Archier ordered the duty officer. "If you find any troops there, tell them to arm themselves. When you've done that, check with the rest of the fleet. I'll go and look into this."

He ran from the Command Centre and back down the broad passageway that led towards the ballroom. But he soon stopped, his blood freezing. Spilling down the corridor, fleeing from the salon, came a panicking mob, a jostling forest of screaming, multicoloured shapes.

Trying to give himself time to think, he pressed himself against the wall as the crowd surged by. How could this horror have come about? *Through the intermats,* she had said. And the kiosks in the salon were only one of several sets throughout the big battleship. But how could rebels have gained access to the intermat facility?

Suddenly he remembered the *Claire de Lune*.

Ragshok was roaring with delight on the mezzanine, clad in a shaggy bearskin coat, the beast's dead snarl a helmet for his skull, a gun in each hand, while turmoil and the satisfying silent flicker of scangun beams filled the music-blasted area below him.

It was incredible. Star Force, terror of the galaxy, dreaded arm of a hard-faced Empire, and here was its real face: a motley of old women (though they seemed trim of figure, he observed), animals and children, and not one of them with the guts to do anything but run and scream.

It would be different with the commando troops, but there probably weren't many of those, and then only on a few ships. He was putting two hundred men and women apiece into *Standard Bearer* and some of the capital ships where he guessed they were stationed. Generally he had to try to take each vessel with only a few dozen.

A sweating Morgan swaggered up in a leather cuirass and tigerskin pants. Ragshok's people often wore animal-derived clothing; it was a way of expressing one's ferocity. In this case Ragshok had ordered them to do so, knowing how much it would dismay and outrage the animals who far outnumbered the humans on the fleet. A good many of *their* hides would be hung out for curing by the end of the day.

"It's a walkover," Morgan said.

"It sure is so far," Ragshok agreed.

To Ikematsu, the change in the mental ambience was instantly obvious. Withdrawing his concentration from the room where Pout and Gruwert conversed, he diffused it, taking in the whole surrounding atmosphere of thought.

The whole ship was in a state of blood-curdling fright, which in the direction of the ballroom was like a thick, clotted mass.

Quickly he spoke to the two boys, pointing down the corridor. "Something bad is happening. Go, and hide yourselves."

Trixa looked bewildered. Sinbiane, attuned to his uncle's perceptions, and used to obeying him instantly, tugged at his friend, urging him to run.

A *kosho* facing danger without his weapons . . . he truly had let himself be put at a disadvantage, Ikematsu thought wryly; and for a second time, and for the same cause.

Stealth would be called for, until he could obtain new weapons . . . Gruwert, he thought then, might know where his own armoury was stored. The pig might be prevailed upon to divulge . . .

As he turned towards the door, it opened and Pout emerged, blinking. Ikematsu's gaze lit upon him, then upon the two boys running down the corridor, then to the end of the corridor.

Not long previously he had fleetingly observed threadlike lines in the air, barely visible. He had taken them for hallucination, a by-product of his mental concentration on radiated thought. But now, approaching from the far end of the corridor, came what looked like a horizontal grid of glistening metal rods. They seemed to move slowly at first, their tips lurching forward, now some in advance, now others, but suddenly they accelerated. The two running boys were momentarily transfixed, and in the same instant they vanished. Then Pout was touched, and vanished.

The rods speared through Ikematsu. He felt nothing, but from the blackness that enveloped him he knew that he, too, had vanished.

CHAPTER TEN

Electric force differs from other forces in having two forms, which conventionally are called positive and negative. Particles bearing the same form of electric charge repel one another, but those bearing opposite charges attract one another.

Actually there is only one fundamental symmetry in nature, and this is the symmetry of left- and right-handedness. 'Charge symmetry' is related to this; it arises because there may be two directions of spin about any axis.

Electric charge originates to begin with when particles within the Hubble sphere are prevented from receding from one another at their natural rate. This puts strain on the recession lines acting between them. The 'thwarted recession' finds its outlet by adopting an angular component. The angular action of all 'strain' lines taken together is called 'pseudospin.' In some ways these 'strain lines' act like lines of force with quasi-material properties. They can even be thought of as 'wrapping around' the particles, though this is not what happens.

To begin with the charge that is thus created is attached to pre-existing particles, but the 'strain space' so created is also capable of generating its own entities consisting purely of electric charge. These are positrons and electrons.

Pseudospin is not like the spin that could be possessed by a material body. To the charged particle itself it would seem that the whole Hubble sphere is rotating around it, not on one axis but on all axes simultaneously. Another strange difference between pseudospin and the spin of a material body is that its sense is absolute, not relative to the observer. If a material disk is set rotating it will appear to be spinning clockwise if looked at from one side but anticlockwise if looked at from the other. Pseudospin, however, will appear to have the same sense of rotation no matter from which side it is looked at. Negative charge will always appear to be clockwise, and positive charge will always appear to be anticlockwise.

Think for a moment what this means. In effect whenever two charged particles interact each selects a direction of spin for the other. Take two electrons. Each electron will look at the other and see clockwise pseudospin. However, seen objectively, i.e. from the standpoint of a third party, the spins that each has selected for the other will be contrary. Likewise an electron will select anticlockwise pseudospin for a proton but the proton will select clockwise pseudospin for the electron. Seen objectively, these spins, though subjectively contrary, have the same sense. Hence it transpires that the rule for electric force is that like attracts like and unlikes repel one another—the opposite of how it appears superficially.

Once the principle of pseudospin is understood it is easy to see how magnetism arises. You have already seen how tilting a spinning gyroscope produces 'gyroscopic action' in which an applied force is turned through a right angle. Every charged particle has attached to it a pseudospin 'gyroscope' the size of the Hubble sphere. Moving the particle is equivalent to tilting that gyroscope . . .

(From *How the World Works*, a physics primer
for young people)

Under the vast spans of Archway City all apparently was at peace. The sky boulevards, beneath which gentle clouds floated, sparkled brilliant as ever. The levitating balconies which were the city's public transport system rose and descended with the same air of leisure. And the air fizzed as ever, laden as it was with billions of tiny popping bubbles containing a mix of psychotropics and pure oxygen.

But within that tranquil architectural grandiosity was an atmosphere of uncertainty and dismay. Imperial Council Member Koutroubis sat in his study, his head in his hands. The study, occupying a location a mile high in one of the shining arches, was open to the air; through its broad windows drifted the cheering bubble fizz, carried on a warm breeze. But it failed to lift the spirits of Koutroubis.

What was he going to tell the Methorians?

They were impatient to depart, waiting only for the data he had promised. But he had been unable to contact the science team that was supposed to be working on the problem of the space rent, or even to ascertain whether it existed!

He felt so helpless!

There was news of disorder in many parts of Diadem, of fighting, even, between Biotists and those loyal to the Council, though he didn't really believe there could have been serious violence. Still, it was lucky they had not brought in the two Star Force fleets, as had been planned. With one on the side of the Council and one on the side of the Biotists, well . . .

He lifted his head in surprise at a banging noise from the direction of the outer door. He heard footsteps in the corridor. Then there barged into the study a lean, agile-looking boar who stopped and darted his gaze ferociously from side to side. Behind him came several more animals and one human, a tall, pale young man in a red cloak.

The boar was Zheikass, Under-Secretary of the Home Star Department and effectively the administrator of affairs in Diadem. The young man was Heskios, a Council Member of junior rank but with no role, as far as Koutroubis could recall, in the Home Star Department. Koutroubis was puzzled. He also recognised two animals beside Zheikass: they were high-ranking civil servants too.

Blankly he addressed his fellow Council member. "Why, Heskios! What are you doing here?"

The other coloured slightly. But his gaze remained stony.

Zheikass spoke, in a stormy squeal. *"Councillor, you are under arrest!"*

Stunned, Koutroubis rose to his feet. Stuttering, he spoke again to Heskios.

"Are you really a party to this?"

"I happen to believe they are right, sir," Heskios replied stiffly.

"And *you*, Zheikass." Koutroubis turned his gaze to the pig. "I never realized *you* were a Whole-Earth-Biotist."

The boar, already a large animal, seemed to swell even larger. He glared in outrage.

"Don't you dare call *me* a Biotist!" he rasped.

In his grief Archier stumbled as he made his way through achingly empty concourses, ruined salons, wide echoing corridors from which bodies had been lately cleared. The air of dereliction was complete. It was as if the flagship, indeed the whole fleet, drifted unmanned.

In fact most of the crew were huddled in their quarters. The orgy of destruction was over, curbed by Ragshok when the two factions among the raiders—formerly defeated rebels, who felt some moral compunction, and outright pirates, who felt none—had begun fighting one another. Much life had been saved thereby, though the wanton killing of animals, which none of the Escorians seemed to recognise as fellow beings, had continued apace.

The helplessness of the ship's crew, once the raiders got aboard, had been nightmarish. No one was armed; even the commandos had been unable to reach their armouries. Still, they had managed to put up a resistance. Many an enemy had fallen to tooth and claw, though in the end this had resulted in savage reprisals.

He swayed, at the top of a gentle slope that led down to what had been, to all intents and purposes, an open-air cafe, bathed in sunlight, a blue sky above. The sunlamp, the hologrammed sky, were smashed. Tables were overturned and bore the dark stains of dried blood.

Suddenly two figures emerged from the interior of the cafe and began to mount the slope. They were Ragshok's men. On their heads were the stolen hats of staff officers. Swarthy muscled bodies showed through skimpy wraps made of animal pelts. Both wore tawny close-fitting pants—lionskin, probably—and carried their scanguns insolently over their loins, like codpieces.

Clearly they had been sampling what the cafe had to offer, for they walked unsteadily as they came up to Archier.

"Eh, it's the Admiral," slurred one. "Howdy, A'm'ral."

The other grabbed Archier by the arm, swung him round and raised a fist to hit him in the face. "Whatcha doin' still alive, Admiral?"

"Leave him alone!"

The peremptory female voice rang out, causing the pirate

to jerk round in surprise. Hesper Positana came striding from the other end of the cafe area. Boldly she climbed the slope and waved the two men back.

"Clear out, or Ragshok will hear of it."

The sight of her black and silver uniform seemed to have an effect on them. One grinned sheepishly.

"All right, sister, keep your vest on."

The phrase was opaque to Archier. He allowed the girl to lead him down the ramp. Behind him, his assailants passed on.

"You'd be safer in your quarters," Hesper told him. "Those two might have killed you if I hadn't happened along."

"This is my fleet," Archier said stubbornly. "My ship." He sighed. "They killed my adjutant," he said blankly. "He was such a nice little chap."

"I'm sorry."

"What are you sorry for?" Archier said dolefully. "You've won. This is what you wanted."

"You'll have to believe me when I say that I never wanted what I've seen happen here. We fought to get you Imperials off our necks, that's all. So as not to have to let our best men and women be carried off to Diadem. Not to have your fleets hovering over our heads threatening to blast us all."

"It looks like you'll have that. But in the process Diadem is going to be ripped apart by these people. It's going to be ghastly."

She looked at him sharply. "You mean you can't defend yourselves?"

He shook his head. "Diadem is wide open. It's completely defenceless."

"But what about the other fleets?"

"They are out in the Empire. They've been ordered to stay out of Diadem, as a matter of fact. There's . . . a political crisis there."

She was silent for a while. "Look," she said at length, "for what it's worth to you, I haven't got any time for these characters. Ragshok's people are just scum. Shipwreckers . . . the ironic thing is, it's the fleets that have prevented us from clearing the spacelanes of these pirates, by not letting us have proper policing forces of our own . . . And though the others wear the same uniform as myself, I don't feel a part of them. They're the dregs of the rebel forces, the garbage."

She stopped in her tracks. "Why, I've seen them rape *children.*"

Despite himself, Archier smiled. "I doubt if what you saw was rape," he said.

The mainly male invaders had, it was clear, come aboard with the intention of making free with the flagship's women. Initially they had been disappointed. All but a handful of the nubile human females followed the fad of facial senility, which the Escorians were unsophisticated enough to find repulsive. When things settled down a little, however, the Priapus' People troupe, including the young girl trainees, had been more than willing to accommodate them.

"I know what I saw," Hesper insisted. "You probably don't understand these things. You people from Diadem are so innocent in some ways. Sex isn't really a part of your lives at all, is it?"

"Well, I wouldn't say . . ."

She was thoughtful, not hearing him. "Isn't there any way to regain control? I mean, I don't want to see the fleet handed back to you, to the Imperials. But I would like to see it in *responsible* Escorian hands. If we had Ten-Fleet we could defend Escoria as a sovereign state, without doing crazy criminal things like rampaging around Diadem." She reflected. "What happened to all the prisoners you took?"

"They're still on the prison ship. Ragshok didn't release them . . . he's ahead of you."

"So? How would *we* go about releasing them?"

Archier found he liked the Escorian girl. He admired her guts. But he shook his head. "There's no way to get to them. The intermats are under guard. The only other way would be to steal a gig, but what with the way Ragshok lets people like me wander around he must be pretty confident that's not possible either."

In fact Archier had been in the Command Centre since the take-over. Ragshok had wanted him to explain how to mesh feetol bubbles and fly the fleet in formation. Although in fear of his life, Archier had refused; but it had made no difference. Handling the fleet was fairly easy, and Ragshok's men had soon got the hang of it. Ten-Fleet was now heading for Diadem at top speed.

He ushered Hesper down a narrow passage that ran just behind the cafe. "Apparently you've been taught certain ideas regarding our attitude to sexuality," he said. "I'd like to show you that those ideas are a misconception. Actually many people in Diadem think provincials can't separate sex from reproduction. You are described as erotically uneducated. But perhaps that's not true either.''

The corridor contained several arched doors. One opened as Archier placed his palm on it. Inside there was only a vague diffused light, until Archier slid the door shut behind them and touched a contact.

At once the room had defined limits. They were surrounded by—themselves; their own images thrown back at them in multiple, from every possible angle, at every stage of enlargement.

He smiled at her as he hit a second contact, flooding the room with aphrodisiac. ''In here is our own universe, consisting only of ourselves.''

Quickly he stripped off, throwing his garments in a corner and moving towards the shell-shaped couch that, reflecting imagery as completely as the walls, floor and ceiling, was almost invisible. His images moved as he moved, piling flesh tone on flesh tone, totally submerging Hesper's vision.

''Why, this is *perverted*,'' *she said delightedly. She was grinning, and the gas was getting to her. Trying to keep her eye on the real Archier amid the image flood, she unpeeled her uniform and stepped from it.*

''*I wanted to thank you for saving my life,*'' Archier said.

The endless mural of writhing limbs and organs engulfed them as they came together.

CHAPTER ELEVEN

The natural colour of this planet's sky was a blue so pale as to be almost white. The sun was large and alum-pale, glaring behind that sky like a ghost of a sun, shimmering, casting a moderate heat.

Hako Ikematsu was interested in neither sky nor sun, but he frequently peered overhead nevertheless. The processes that took place in the sky, in the air, sometimes reaching down to the ground, were interesting indeed.

They were, of course, the same as had appeared on board ICS *Standard Bearer,* but here the range of their operations was easier to view. It was rather as if the space near the planet had been engulfed in a sort of linear cobweb which entered the atmosphere occasionally, blown by a cosmic wind. Long glistening threads, always dead straight, always parallel. He had, of course, guessed the nature of those threads, ever since being transposed, in the twinkling of an eye, from the corridor in the flagship to the surface of this world.

It was surprising he was still in one piece. He suspected he would not be so for long if those threads should touch him again. In the days that the weaponless *kosho* had been searching for his nephew he had come upon the remains of numbers of people, beasts, buildings and artifacts. In every case they had been dismantled; not clumsily, as a butcher or a demolitioner would do it, but with extraordinary finesse. In the case of the organic remnants there was often remarkably little blood. Separations were apt to be along natural lines of division: membranes, sinews, systemic functions. Nerves were left dangling, sometimes pulled out of their ensheathing flesh to a length of several feet, or with receptor organs still attached. How such careful dissection had been accomplished, by beings who did not even seem to be beings, and who lacked any apparent means of manipulation, was a mystery.

Neither did the disassemblers seem to be able to differentiate between what was organic and what was not. Besides separated limbs and organs, Ikematsu had seen bits of machinery carefully laid out as if ready for assembly, and whole buildings unfolded like packing cases and laid flat. Even stretches of landscape had been pulled apart and rearranged, leaving weird patterns in soil, vegetation and concrete.

The agents of these mutilations were not hard to identify. Ikematsu paused, his shrewd brown eyes intent, as they came down again, the limitlessly lengthening lines slanting down like hawsers of steel sunlight. The cluster stroked the landscape midway to the horizon. It was moving sidewise, progressing towards him.

Uncharacteristically Ikematsu tensed. But the lines vanished, as quickly as they had come.

He continued on his way. This region appeared to have been thinly populated. So far he had found no one left alive apart from himself. But he would not rest until he knew what had happened to Sinbiane, even though there was no guarantee that the boy had materialised anywhere near him—or, indeed, that he had rematerialised at all.

A road ran from planetary west to east through meadows of bluish grass. A mile away to the west he saw a solitary house—the first standing building he had see for some time.

He reached it in half an hour, approaching slowly and cautiously, to find that it was no more than a cottage. In a neatly tended garden furniture had been tumbled, mixed amid flowers and miniature trees.

Ikematsu knocked on a door panel, finding no call plate. When there was no answer he attempted to slide the panel aside; it failed to yield. He pushed it; it swung inward upon hinges.

He stepped directly into an empty room illuminated by a wide one-way window. The *kosho* halted. So as to be able to take in the nature of this room, he suspended all emotional reaction.

A blue eye, distinctly human, stared at him from the surface of the wall opposite. In the wall to his right two equally human brown eyes were similarly embedded, but separated by a distance of about ten feet, one near the ceiling, the other, placed vertically, in the corner near the floor.

The match to the blue eye Ikematsu found near the door jamb.

But not until he had seen much else. There were human

fragments fused throughout the walls, floor and ceiling. Ears, toes, fingers and young male genitals sprouted like pale fruits. Here and there the surfaces bulged, in shapes resembling a heart, a liver, or a pelvic bone.

And running throughout walls, floor and ceiling, like an embossed design, were tiny pipelike protrusions: arteries and veins. Ikematsu stepped closer, inspecting the glistening surface. He saw a faint tracery, spreading over the wall like fronds.

Nerves.

Suddenly a whispering, muffled voice came from somewhere. "Uncle! This is me, Sinbiane! I am alive!"

"Sinbiane!"

"Yes, uncle, I am here. And Trixa too."

"You can see me?"

"Yes."

Ikematsu took up a position in the centre of the room and stared straight into the blue eye, paradoxically aware that Sinbiane must thereby have a double view of him, both front and back. "Tell me what you understand of your situation," he ordered.

"I know what has happened, uncle," the hidden voice said. "Our bodies have been dispersed throughout the walls of this cottage. It is a strange experience. I am wrapped right round you. With each eye I look at the other eye."

"Is there any pain?"

"No, not even hunger."

"What of your mental condition?"

"I am all right, uncle. I have stayed collected. But if we get out of here my friend will need considerable psychological help. He is in a state of total shock."

"That is because he lacks mental training."

Taking care where he trod, Ikematsu moved to the window and looked out. The sky was clear of alien rods.

Briefly he reflected. Apparently the intruders from the other facet were not content with simple analysis; they were trying to manipulate the world more positively.

It was remarkable that they were able to disperse the boys' bodies while still maintaining the integrity of all the somatic systems, particularly the vascular and nervous systems. It said much for their own mode of perception.

"Uncle," Sinbiane said, "*can* we be restored to what we were before?"

"Yes, you can," Ikematsu told him. "The surgeons on the

Imperial fleet would be able to put you back together again. But that will depend on their recovering this planet. At the moment when the aliens snatched us away, the flagship was under attack and had been boarded. If others have taken control of the fleet they will have moved it out of the danger area by now.''

To that, Sinbiane was silent. ''I have no intention of lying to you,'' Ikematsu said. ''Meantime you have a rare opportunity to practise mental flexibility. It should stand you in good stead when you train to become a *kosho*.''

''I never imagined anything like this happening, uncle.''

''I hope you do not expect the world to be limited by your imagination, nephew.''

Ikematsu paused again, still thinking. ''Is there anything you can tell me about the beings who did this, or how they did it?'' he asked Sinbiane.

''It happened so quickly, uncle. It was all over in a moment. But I seemed to gain a mental impression of them. They are very confused. They don't understand our world, but they are trying to understand it. That is why they did this. They don't realize they are meddling with living beings.''

''They have no conception of discrete objects,'' Ikematsu agreed. ''That is deducible from their own manifestations.'' In fact, he told himself, an act of this kind was probably not even possible in 'normal' space. They had brought their own kind of space with them. That was what appeared as the extending lines or threads.

''Did you see the animal, Pout?'' Sinbiane asked.

''No,'' Ikematsu replied quickly, immediately interested. ''Why do you ask?''

''He was here too. He cannot be far away.''

''Was the same thing done to him?''

''I do not know. But I don't think he is here in the house.''

''I am leaving now to find the chimera,'' Ikematsu said. ''I will return when I am able. Meantime, do not shame my abilities as an instructor by losing courage.''

Sinbiane did not reply as he strode from the room.

It did not take long to locate Pout. The chimera was but a few yards farther down the road, partly hidden in a thicket of coarse long-stemmed plants.

He was, in fact, incorporated into one of the plants, or vice versa. He was jammed in a squatting position, while the stems, entering at his buttocks, merged with his legs, his arms and his torso, emerging at knees, elbows, and through his abdomen and thorax. A large, yellow-petalled flower seemed to frame his face.

His face. It was his face that rivetted Ikematsu's attention, while the chimera squirmed in dumb distress, glaring with huge piteous eyes. For in that face, set into it as if set in blancmange, was the zen gun. The gun *was* his face, or a part of it. The barrel jutted straight out in place of a nose, waving and poking towards Ikematsu, making the whole visage hatchet-shaped. The stock merged with and disappeared into Pout's pendulous mouth.

After studying the spectacle Ikematsu leaned towards the chimera, hands on hips. "How you loved your toy! Now it is truly yours. But do you still want it?"

Pout waved his head vigorously from side to side, making the yellow petals shake as if in a storm. A howling wave of rejection emanated from his crazed brain.

"NO GUN! NO GUN!"

"If I succeed in relieving you of it, will you concede that the gun becomes mine? You must grant it to me willingly. Otherwise it stays attuned to you."

The effort of communicating to Ikematsu seemed to have exhausted Pout. He sagged, sucking air into his throat round the intruding stock that nearly blocked his mouth. Slowly, his head nodded.

"Good . . ." Ikematsu mused. "But how is it to be done . . .?"

Tentatively he reached out a hand, touching the wooden barrel. Seizing it between thumb and finger, he tugged experimentally.

Almost without resistance, the gun slid out of Pout's face. There was a *plop* as his features re-formed behind it.

Pout began to cry.

At last, *kosho* Hako Ikematsu permitted himself to exult, at last he held the zen gun in his hands.

Zen in the art of electronics . . .

Curiously there was no trace of its contact with the interior of Pout's person. No slime or moisture. No body heat, only the ordinary cool warmth of friendly wood. Ikematsu turned it over and over, examining it at length.

He knew its age: more than three Earth centuries. He knew

its provenance: the zen master who made it had been a member of the order from which his own had originally sprung. The external appearance of the gun was a testament to certain cultural concepts: it seemed improvised, unfinished, crude, yet in its lack of polish was a feeling of supreme skill . . . in the Nipponese language of the time it had *wabi*, the quality of artless simplicity, the rustic quality of leaves strewn on a path, of a gate mended roughly with a nailed-on piece of wood and yet whose repair was a quiet triumph of adequacy and conscious balance. It had *shibusa*, the merit of imperfection. Only incompleteness could express the infinite, could convey the essence of reality. Hence, the unvarnished wood bore the marks of the carver's chisel . . .

These qualities were themselves but superficial excrescences of the principles on which the gun acted, principles so abstruse in character that one dictum alone succeeded in hinting at them: *Nothing moves. Where would it go?* Pout the chimera had succeeded in using the gun as an electric beam to hurt or kill, without regard to location. But that was the most trivial of its capabilities. Only a *kosho* could unlock its real, dreadful purpose . . .

CHAPTER TWELVE

Ragshok's voice was slurred as he spoke to Archier. He had not been able to resist the intoxicating airs and beverages so freely available on the flagship.

"We'll be in Diadem in less then two days," he said. "Listen, you could be useful to us. Tell us which are the juiciest worlds. Where we'd go to forestall resistance."

"I'm your prisoner, that's all," Archier said dully. "Don't expect me to be a traitor as well."

Ragshok took a long sucking drag on the foot-long charge cigar he was smoking. He grinned glassily at Hesper. "Work on him, love. Make him see the light. Simplex take it! I can offer you *anything*. Wanna be total dictator of a hundred worlds? Satisfy any kink you like? Come on, everybody's got his price!"

Hesper snuggled closer to Archier and stared at the pirate distastefully.

"Aaargh . . ." Ragshok growled in his throat, his natural aggressiveness overcoming even the calming effect of the drug. "Who needs you, hn? Who needs you?"

The door slid open with a bang. Ragshok turned, eyebrows lifted, as someone burst into the small sitting room where they were talking. It was one of the women in his band, a middle-aged virago who had been particularly bloodthirsty during the takeover. Her face was ugly with alarm.

"There's a fleet ahead of us, chief!"

"What are you talking about?" Ragshok's surprise was almost comic. He took the cigar out of his mouth, rolling it between thumb and finger.

"It's on the radar. A big Imperial fleet!"

Grumbling incoherently to himself, Ragshok lurched to his feet. He pointed to Archier. "Bring him to the Command Room."

He ran through the door. Archier didn't need the scangun

that was pointed at his head to persuade him to follow. He went willingly, and in the Command Centre found Ragshok already on the throne, his lieutenants, Morgan included, grouped around him. In the air in front of them there hovered the radar report.

There was no doubt of it. The oncoming blips were in standard Star Force formation, and there were more of them than Ten-Fleet could currently boast. In fact, from the identifying symbols in the top left of the image Archier knew it to be Seventeen-Fleet.

Swivelling the throne, Ragshok glared at Archier. "So this is what you've been keeping quiet," he accused, speaking the words round the huge, puffing cigar. "Diadem *is* defended."

"I don't really understand it," Archier admitted mildly. "No fleets are stationed in Diadem. The last I heard, Star Force had been ordered to stay away altogether." He smiled faintly. "That's Seventeen-Fleet coming at us, and she's nearly up to strength. You'd better surrender. Maybe you'll be treated leniently—given remedial treatment, given homes in Diadem, even."

"Made tax slaves, you mean. They haven't even attacked yet, and they won't when we put you onscreen to reassure them."

"I'm afraid they will, whatever you make me say. We're supposed to be somewhere else. Remember those funny cobweb things that were making people disappear? We are supposed to be investigating that. Turning up like this makes us look like a threat. You see," he explained after hesitation, "there's been a civil conflict inside Diadem. They probably think we're aiming to mix in it. They must think it, in fact, or they wouldn't be coming out to meet us."

The radar picture suddenly disintegrated into a three-dimensional cross-hatchwork. Then the operators briefly obtained a single magnified image of one of the dreadful front-line-o'-wars, already extending its immensely long gun barrels.

"They outgun us," Ragshok muttered.

"Fight 'em, chief!" Morgan urged. "We've got plenty of guns too. They don't outgun us *all* that much."

"They know how to use what they've got, you fool, and we don't!" Ragshok retorted. He took the cigar from his mouth and flung it away. "We'll be smashed to pieces if we stay in formation like this. Order the fleet to disperse. Every

ship to avoid contact as best it can and make its own way into
Diadem. We can exert some leverage there. Civilians are
always soft-bellied.''

When he heard this, Archier's jaw dropped. ''You don't
know what you're doing!'' he yelled.

''SHUT UP! Get him out of here!''

He heard the order being relayed and was still protesting as
the virago hustled him from the room. Outside, he stared
blankly at the lens of the scangun she held on him. How
much should he exert himself, risk his life even, for the sake
of these people?

It was a grotesque death. But he would get his fleet back . . .

He remained wrestling with his conscience when she
vanished, with a clap of air.

For a while he stood there. Then, slowly, he walked back
into the Command Centre. It was empty, of course. With a
dazed feeling, he took up the throne so precipitously vacated
by Ragshok.

Hesper found him there a few minutes later, having followed at her own pace. ''Where are they all?'' she asked.

''Back in the *Claire de Lune*,'' Archier told her dully.
''But dead, of course.''

While she continued to stare at him in mystification, he
waved at the radar picture. ''Do you see that? It's another
Imperial fleet on its way to intercept us. To escape it Ragshok
decided to scatter Ten-Fleet. But he didn't understand about
the intermat, you see. I don't suppose hardly anybody outside
Star Force does.

''You see, the intermat only works inside the big feetol
bubble that encloses the fleet when it's flying in what we call
feetol formation. And it isn't really permanent. You have to
return to your point of origin before the bubble disappears,
otherwise you'll transpose back there spontaneously, in a
horribly mangled state because there's no intermat kiosk to
regulate the process. That's what happened when Ragshok
dispersed the fleet and burst the bubble. Remember, his
people had spread themselves around the fleet by intermat in
the first place. I don't like to think what it must look like on
the *Claire de Lune* right now.''

He wasn't sure Hesper took in what he said about the feetol
bubble, but she was bright enough to grasp the bottom line.
''You mean *all* Ragshok's people have been killed?'' she
said. ''*All* of them?''

"All except the handful who stayed aboard *Claire de Lune* from the beginning. Some of my own people must have got caught, too," he brooded. "Not everybody managed to get back to their own vessels after the takeover."

He sighed. "Better get on to Seventeen, I suppose, before they blast us out of the galaxy."

Using his Admiral's throne codes to override the crewless space torsion room, he succeeded in sending a leader tone burst to the flagship of the approaching fleet. Once contact was made the signal was good; they were only minutes away from gunnery range.

In the other's torsion room, he found himself looking into the mild face of a koala. "This is Admiral Archier," he announced. "Would you please put me through to Admiral Tirexier."

"Admiral Brusspert now has command, sir. I will try to get him for you."

Brusspert? Archier frowned. He knew no such admiral. Very likely he or she was a promotion . . . but surely Tirexier was not suspected of disloyalty? He could no more believe it of him than he would of himself.

He thought the koala had made a mistake when a grinning pig face confronted him. The pig wore something on its head: it was with a shock that he recognised it, after a moment, as an adaptation of the ceremonial admiral's hat, with its peaked, bell-shaped dome.

"Ah, there you are, Archier. Now then, what the Simplex do you think you're doing?"

"Do I address Admiral Brusspert?" Archier asked after a pause.

"Indeed, indeed. Now come to it! Our gunners are raring to go! You saw Crane and Oblescu, I suppose?"

Archier swallowed. As concisely as he could, he related everything that had taken place. When he had finished, Brusspert sniffed dubiously.

"A pretty unlikely tale in the circumstances, I must say . . . Still, we'll confirm the truth, or otherwise, of it sharp enough." The pig's eyes flickered to something in his range of vision. "Your ships don't behave as though they have anyone at the helm, at that. Zipping about like a bunch of pesky swamp flies. We'll chase them down and board. Meantime, make ready to receive our gig. We're coming over."

"First," Archier said, "may I ask how a second class citizen comes to have the rank of admiral? Yours *is* an *acting* rank, I take it?"

Brusspert stared at him. Then he broke into squealing laughter. "You haven't heard, then? Don't worry, you'll find out soon enough!"

The picture vanished. The new admiral had cut him off.

In the short interval before the gig from Seventeen Fleet arrived Archier made some attempt to put his flagship back in order. He called the living quarters and informed the vessel's denizens that it was safe to come out. Slowly the ship began to fill with sounds of life, and he was surprised once again to see his Fire Command Officer, whom he had presumed killed along with so many other animals. It transpired that Gruwert had spent the last few days hiding in a locker, and had ventured forth only when he heard voices he recognised. Thinner, and somewhat bad-tempered, he gulped down an enormous quantity of his favourite mash, and then reported for duty.

Archier was not sure what it would be like to confront a pig admiral. There was an ingrained protocol for dealing with animals. He did not go to the boarding bay to meet the gig, as he might normally have done, but waited in his office for the party to come to him.

It was larger than he had expected: about twenty animals and humans, though few of the latter. Half a dozen of them trotted into his office, and all of them were four-footed.

He had not realized earlier that Admiral Brusspert was a sow. Her plump danging udders were evidence that she had littered recently. Archier noted the fact only in passing. It was swallowed up in his general shock.

"Admiral," she announced with a toss of her snout, "permit me to introduce Imperial Council Member Hiroshamak."

Standing beside her was indeed someone in a Council Member's robe, but instead of hanging with loose dignity from a pair of shoulders, it had been cut and shaped so as to drape upon the broad back of a quadruped.

Imperial Council Member Hiroshamak, also, was a pig.

Archier swayed, then fell back into his chair. "So the Council has been overthrown," he gasped softly. "Revolution!"

"Do not distress yourself, Admiral," Hiroshamak said in gruff but resonant tones. "The Council still rules: there has been no revolution, at least not of the kind you mean. If you are truly loyal to the Empire, you should be pleased by the turn of events.''

He started to pace up and down. Archier could not help but notice the personal charisma of the animal, the sense of purpose and restless energy. ''Let me put this to you, Admiral. For a long time now it has mainly been we pigs who have been propping up the Empire. To put it bluntly, we are more capable than other animals—just as capable as humans, in fact. Implanted intelligence works particularly well with us. But unlike humans, *we* have not lost interest in the well-being of the Empire. We have not become, if you don't mind me saying so, effete, incompetent and short-sighted. In addition, we breed at a healthy rate and so there are plenty of us! You will grant that all this is so.''

''Oh yes,'' Archier said faintly. ''My pigs have always been most efficient. And resourceful.''

''I'm glad you agree. The truth is that again and again the senior pig administrators in the civil service have had to rescue the Imperial Council from the consequences of its own bungling. Left to its own devices, it would have wrecked the Empire on a dozen occasions over the past few years. Well, things have simply been going from bad to worse. The present crisis finally convinced us that matters can no longer be left to human ineptness. We have found it necessary to act— with a small measure of illegality, regrettably, but that has been kept to a minimum . . . Not to put too fine a point on it, the entire membership of the Imperial Council has been 'persuaded' to resign. A new Council has been appointed, consisting entirely of pigs. Like myself, they are mostly drawn from the higher ranks of the civil service.''

''Second class,'' Archier muttered in bewilderment. ''You are second-class citizens. It isn't possible . . .''

''Not any longer. We have introduced a second innovation. Since the pigs are now to play such a prominent part in the affairs of the Empire, they have been elevated to first-class citizenship alongside humans. We are now equals in law.

''If you think about it,'' the pig continued as Archier struggled to absorb what he was being said to him, ''I'm sure you'll realize it's the only way. Only forthright measures will restore the Empire's fortunes, and the simple fact is that humans have become too accustomed to hesitancy and weakness. Let me give you some idea of the programme we pigs have adopted.''

Hiroshamak raised a trotter in the air and counted off points with it. ''One: recalcitrant or tax-defaulting worlds to be destroyed promptly and without warning as an example to others. Two: all striking robots to be exterminated and a new class, with lower intelligence and no political aspirations, to be manufactured. These will begin work immediately on replacement war fleets to bring Star Force up to strength. Three: human immigration into Diadem to be forcibly increased for work in laboratories or where creative effort is required, also to supplement the robot labour force if the new brand of robot proves too low-grade for skilled work. These new immigrants will have no citizenship rights at all to begin with. They will have to earn them. That way they can be stopped from running out on us.''

''But that would make them slaves!'' Archier protested.

''Slave, slave! It's only a word. This attitude of yours is exactly what's been wrong with our political position up until now. These measures are necessary, but I grant it takes a certain amount of determination to apply them. That is what humans appear to lack.''

''But there's a *reason* why animals were made second-class citizens,'' Archier objected earnestly. ''Animals don't have creative minds!''

''I acknowledge that,'' Hiroshamak said instantly, ''but it doesn't matter a damn! Governing an Empire doesn't call for creativity—it was a misconception ever to think that it does. Shrewdness, cunning and self-confidence are what's needed. We pigs have proved ourselves there.''

''Society *needs* creativity,'' Archier insisted. ''It's what keeps it evolving.''

''Of course. Who doubts it? And that's exactly the role we see humans filling in the new dispensation. Creative thought— art, science, the things they are good at. And we'll take care of practical affairs.''

Admiral Brusspert interrupted him enthusiastically. Only now did Archier spot the feminine difference in her voice tone. It never was very noticeable in porcines. ''Absolutely right, Council Member,'' she said. ''Pigs make the right decisions! The weasels, for instance—tell him about that!''

''Weasels?'' Archier enquired.

"Guard!" Hiroshamak snapped in answer. "Get in here sharpish!"

Into the room, walking on its hind legs, came a five-foot stoat in military accoutrement. The scangun at its waist was adapted to fit its paw. Its backpack, breathing kit and communicator made it look even more predatory.

"He's had his inhibitor removed," Hiroshamak said.

Now Archier was not merely shocked. He was aghast. Of all the mammals in the commonalty, there was one family that was never used in war: the weasel family, including stoats, polecats, wolverines and fishers. Tigers and bears were as nothing to the mad ferocity of these creatures. They were the most gifted murder machines nature had devised, restricted only by their size—wolverines and fishers, in fact, would unhesitatingly attack and kill anything they came across, no matter how large. That was why intelligent weasels were given additional implants to repress their savage urges, and why wolverines and fishers were very rarely made intelligent at all.

"You are seeing the backbone of the future Drop Commando," Hiroshamak informed Archier. "Tell him how you feel without the inhibitor, guard."

Archier could almost see the stoat smile. "Much better, sir. Much sharper. And more ready to serve the Empire, sir, of course."

"All right, guard. That will do. Wait outside."

"The old Council never need bodyguards," Archier remarked when the predator had gone.

"Oh, I don't suppose we will when things have settled down."

"There's something I must ask you." Archier swallowed. "Are you Biotists? You must be, since you want to dethrone man from his superior position—"

"No, no, we are not Biotists." Hiroshamak and Brusspert both shook their heads emphatically. "It was partly to stop the Biotists taking over that we acted as we did! Like them, we assert that the Empire belongs to *all* mammals, not merely to humans. But we shall never recommence gene mixing. The species should stay separate. It's the best way of standardising intelligence." Hiroshamak's eyes twinkled. "Besides, we like being pigs!"

"What happened to Admiral Tirexier?" Archier asked suddenly, with a bite in his voice."

"Ah yes. You force me to a delicate matter," Hiroshamak replied after a pause. "A new High Command is being organised. The new command structure is to consist entirely of pigs, and affects all ranks from admiral up. That means, Admiral Archier, that you are being retired from active service as an admiral. You will retain the rank of Admiral retired, of course, and you will continue to serve in the fleet in a lower acting capacity. Your Fire Command Officer Gruwert is being promoted in your place. You have always commended his initiative."

A squeal of delight sounded behind Archier. It came from Gruwert, who together with others of the Command Staff had been standing silently listening to the exchange.

"Yes, I have," whispered Archier. "Indeed I have."

Carefully he removed his admiral's ceremonial hat, with its bell-shaped crown, its glittering feathers, and placed it on his desk.

My fleet, he thought agonisedly. *My beautiful Ten-Fleet.*

But of course it was not his fleet, and never had been. It was the Empire's, and now the Empire belonged to the pigs.

Gruwert came trotting forward, snuffing the air. "No hard feelings, Archier old chap? It's all for the best, you know. Now if you don't mind, I'd like you to get out of my office. It's time to start doing things properly!"

CHAPTER THIRTEEN

At last Admiral Gruwert felt he had a proper outlet for his energies. He was enjoying his new role immensely.

Lifting his snout from the trough of choice delicacies he had installed in his office, he returned his attention to his duties.

The fleet was very nearly restored to operational status and was heading at top speed for Axaline Sector, the region it had been forced to quit when summoned to Escoria. Imperial Council Member Hiroshamak had given Gruwert explicit orders: there were signs that Axaline felt encouraged by recent events, not to revolt exactly, but to mount a campaign of stubborn civil disobedience, and the sector was to be discouraged by peremptory means.

The Axalines would find their error of judgment a most costly one. Gruwert recalled the planet Rostia. They would get no reprieve this time, he promised himself with satisfaction. It would be knuckle under *at once* or—

A voice interrupted his scanning of the weapons readiness reports. It was the new pig brigadier he had put in charge of the Drop Commando.

"Admiral, something odd is happening. One or two rebel pirates have been turning up. I thought they had all been dealt with."

"Eh?" Gruwert thought quickly. "What have you done with them?"

"Scanned them away, naturally."

Gruwert muttered under his breath. He was annoyed, while at the same time pleased that the Commandos were as keen as ever. They were armed permanently now, and stationed as a guard force throughout every ship of the fleet. It had not been lost on Gruwert that there might be internal dissension to deal with—indeed, he would not feel entirely safe until he re-

ceived postings of some of the newly trained weasels whose
loyalty was guaranteed.

"Don't scan them," he ordered. "If you find any more,
take them alive. They're probably the ones who started disappearing shortly after we were boarded. Remember? Those
funny lines in the air? It was the space rent doing it." He
reflected again. "Some of our own people vanished too . . .
leave that in my hands."

"Yes sir."

Gruwert cursed briefly as the Brigadier broke contact. Why
did the Drop Commando have to bring him this news? It
should have been picked up by Archier, the new Ship Management Officer! At any rate, he would need Archier to survey
the ship's population and see if any vanished personnel had
reappeared.

He put out a call to Archier. To his fury, there was no
answer. The man wasn't contactable!

Such incompetence was all too believable! He would have
him demoted yet again! He would have him cleaning the
decks with the robots! The pesky human!

Gruwert suppressed his anger for long enough to think. The
threat from the rent in space still remained. The Imperial
Council was supposed to be organising a special scientific
organisation to deal with it, but Star Force wasn't involved.
Gruwert got the impression the Council was hoping the rent
would go away on its own, which he didn't really think was
the right attitude.

If people really were reappearing from wherever it was
they had vanished to, they probably had some valuable
information.

He heaved himself to his trotters, telling his adjutant to stay
where he was. Nothing like a personal appearance to an
awkward moment for keeping the staff on their toes . . .

Fleet Admiral (Retired) Archier, now Acting Ship Management Officer, sat disconsolately holding hands with Hesper
Positana. She had discarded her rebel's uniform, after he had
persuaded her that transportation to Diadem would not, any
longer, mean a life of luxury and leisure. Instead, he had
contrived to place her on the ship's register.

"How could the humans among you let it *happen?*" she
protested.

She still did not understand about Diadem. "It just happened," he said simply.

"But they're not *people*. They're pigs. *Pigs!*"

"They *are* people, Hesper. To us, animals are people as well as human beings."

"Well they're not very *nice* people, are they?"

He was silent. He hardly dared mention what the future almost certainly held. A pig-ruled galaxy. A tyranny, probably, in which humans might even be relegated to second-class citizenship eventually. He was sure the pigs would never agree to share power with humans again, no matter what they said at present. The future belonged to them. They alone had the crude self-confidence that was needed, the ruthlessness, the love of power.

Neither did he believe the coup had been as bloodless as Hiroshamak claimed. There must have been opposition. It looked, now, as if they had actually used the fleets. All except Ten-Fleet had been taken over simultaneously by senior pig officers. Obviously, then, there had been a deal of forward planning. Probably Gruwert and his pig pals had been waiting for a signal too . . .

"There's talk of other species getting first-class citizenship too, if they prove themselves," he remarked emptily.

"The weasels, most probably! They'll grant them privileges, to make them even more enthusiastic." Hesper squeezed his hand and leaned closer. "Just what *is* your loyalty to?" she asked anxiously. "Is it to the Empire, no matter *who* owns it? Or to mankind, and civilisation?"

"Need civilisation be man's alone?"

"Yes!" she said emphatically. "Because only man is truly intelligent. These animals of yours—the only intelligence they have is what *you* gave them. It's borrowed. Apart from that, they're still undeveloped—not really sentient."

Archier listened carefully to her words. They sounded novel and strange. Was this how people in the provinces thought?

He sighed. "I don't know what you woud have me do, Hesper. The pigs are in an invulnerable position. There's scarcely any opposition that I've noticed among the flagship staff, and they are the most dedicated citizens in the Empire. In fact, I believe they welcome the pigs' coup. The pigs will make the Empire strong again. Strong enough to claim the undisputed allegiance of every inhabited world. Strong enough eventually to embrace the whole galaxy—every biota-compatible planet. That's what the people who run Star Force want, both men and animals.''

"That's right, SMO," said a lusty voice.

It was Gruwert. He came waddling forward, having apparently caught Archier's last words. "It's good you agree things have taken a turn for the better. But keep your communicator active in future, SMO. I've been looking for you."

He swung on Hesper, peering at her. "I don't believe I recognise you, my dear. What's your section?"

"She's in my department, Admiral," Archier said quickly, noting with alarm the loathing with which Hesper stared back at his superior officer.

"And a most touching scene the two of you were putting on, if I may say so. Not showing a lack of, shall we say, *enthusiasm* for the new order, is she? If so you'd better talk some sense into her. Disloyalty won't be tolerated!" His voice rose as he said this and he glared hard at Hesper. "What's the matter with you? Don't you want the Empire to be mighty, triumphant? The whole galaxy belongs to us of right, and it will all have to be held together. So make up your mind to it, because nothing can stop us now."

"Something *can* stop you, animal."

They turned on hearing the softly spoken words. A figure in a loose white garment was framed in the entrance to the chamber. The newcomer gazed on the scene as though not really seeing it, as though staring over their heads at something in the distance. Hesper recognised that look from her previous acquaintance with him. She knew he was observing them all keenly.

"Why, it's the *kosho*," Gruwert squealed in surprise. "I thought the pirates had killed you, *kosho*, or else the rent had taken you. Together with your master, the excellent Pout. What *did* happen to him?"

"He is safe," Ikematsu said blandly. "He is on this ship somewhere. I saw him briefly, but he ran away from me. Yes, the rent took us. But we have returned. Everyone has returned."

Gruwert's eyes narrowed. He had been looking for Pout ever since taking command.

He switched his communicator to subvocal mode and spoke to his adjutant. "That man-ape, Pout. He's on the ship, probably near where I am—I'm in the Ship Management Office. Have him found and brought to me."

"You speak to someone," Ikematsu said knowingly. He stepped into the room and beckoned behind him. Through the door came Sinbiane, leading Trixa by the hand and murmuring encouragement to him. The Diademian boy did not seem to know where he was. His eyes were glazed. His shoulders slumped.

Placing his hand on Sinbiane's shoulder, Ikematsu addressed the pig. "I hear I should congratulate you on a new appointment. No doubt you are now even more anxious to have the chimera under your control. You suspected him of being the weapon that could destroy the Empire. How nearly right you were, pig. But the weapon is neither a new leader or a social idea, as you thought. That was a clever deduction, but the truth is simpler. Remember what the oracle said: *'It has been disregarded because it is small.'* The ultimate weapon is in fact that little gun that Pout carries."

"That *toy?*" Gruwert exploded. "What nonsense is this?"

The *kosho*, his bearing erect and with the odd stylised quality Hesper had often noticed, stepped away from the boys and swivelled to speak to all the three others present. The pig stiffened, his snout following him suspiciously.

"That electric pistol incorporates the most complete understanding of the laws of nature ever attained," Ikematsu said. "It was made by a master of my order centuries ago, for a single reason: to render centrally governed empires impossible.

"The weapon was to accomplish this in a manner quite easy to understand. The zen gun, as it is called, is a sun-destroying handgun. *To one qualified in its use* the procedure is as follows. First, the gunman must get within three light years of the sun to be attacked. He then lines up the barrel with the target, and adjusts the beam so that it will spread to encompass the whole star. He then squeezes the trigger stud.

"The target star is disrupted by electrical means. As you know, positive and negative electricity differs only in the direction of the pseudo-spin of which electric force is composed. The zen gun, delving into the Simplex, inverts the pseudo-spin of all positive charges within the star, switching them to negative. A negligible amount of energy is involved in this simple but remarkable process. You may easily reason out the results. Since both electrons and protons now possess negative charge, there is repulsion both between the nuclei and electron shells of atoms, and between the nuclei of atoms. The star explodes. The electrons, with smaller mass, acquire the higher velocity. An expanding electron cloud totalling one four-thousandth of the mass of the whole star sweeps through the planetary system, ripping off atmospheres and destroying all life.

"The charge inversion lasts only seconds: the imbalance in the constituted universe cannot be maintained for longer than that. Anti-protons become protons again. But it is too late, the separation between charges has been accomplished. Some of the expanding electron cloud is attracted back to the main mass, but not enough to cancel the net positive charge on the more slowly exploding mass of atomic nuclei. In hours the positive cloud, the whole remaining mass of the star, has engulfed and disintegrated every planet of the system. It is millions of years before it attracts enough negative charge to become electrically neutral again. By that time it is too dispersed to coalesce. It never again becomes a star.

"So if you see that happening to a star within your territory, pig, you will know that you have received a warning and that the next sun to go will be the one illuminating your seat of government. The explosion is easily distinguishable from a nova or supernova. First there is a brilliant flash as the trapped photons ricocheting within the star are released. After that the star goes out, because as its stripped atomic nuclei recede from one another nuclear fusion ceases."

Gruwert had been listening to the *kosho*'s story with intent concentration. Now he snorted, his little eyes glittering.

"This is not new. There already are ways to destroy stars."

"With a *handgun?* No, only by moving titanic pieces of apparatus and colossal power sources close to the star—what enemy stands by and allows you to do that? Until now it has never been possible to destroy suns as an act of war. What makes the zen gun invincible is that it is small. One man can carry it unseen, it cannot be kept track of or detected. It is the equaliser between the individual and all the rest of the civilised universe. With just a sidearm, one man can now defeat an empire."

The pig trembled slightly. Head lowered, he glared directly at Ikematsu. He looked as if he were about to charge at him. He had done a wise thing, Gruwert told himself, in bringing his bodyguard along. The stoat was stationed within call just up the corridor.

"*Kosho*, you speak treason, and shortly I shall have you arrested. Are you telling me *you* have this gun?"

"No, I do not have it. I had it, but I lost it."

Gruwert snorted disdainfully. "This tale is preposterous. I do not believe a word of it. The man-ape's toy is only a piece of wood."

"Your disbelief will hasten the triumph of right," Ikematsu responded blandly. "Before the chimera arrives, let me tell you something of the gun's recent history. It may convince you.

"One gun is all that was ever made. Shortly after its manufacture my order was destroyed, in its original form, by political events. The weapon was lost, irrevocably, it was thought.

"Then, a few years ago, a *kosho* by the name of Orohisho Smith succeeded in finding it. Smith was not advanced enough spiritually to decode the gun fully, however. I do not think he was even interested in its ultimate use, only to exploit some of the secondary capabilities its mode of operation entails. Specifically, he wished to explore other facets of the Simplex. As a result of his meddling, the gun opened up the rent in space.

"Smith was never to know what he had done in his ignorance. He was tricked and made prisoner by one Torth Nascimento, who wished to keep him as a human specimen in a museum. To rob this man of his satisfaction, Smith took the course of self-destruction. Meantime his weapons, including the zen gun, had been placed in the museum's weapons section, from where it was stolen by your friend Pout the chimera.

"It was then that I attached myself to Pout. My interest has been to see the gun fall into worthy hands, but I was honour-bound not to take it from him by force. Surprisingly, the gun responded to Pout a little. He was able to employ it as an anti-personnel weapon, and to give him personal power over others. He never guessed at its real secrets, of course. But he used to play with its settings. By doing this he unknowingly broke the gravitational bond between the planet Earth and its large satellite.

Hesper, who with Archier had been listening in silence, gasped. "Is *that* what happened?"

"I don't understand this," Archier said. "There *is* no actual bond between gravitating bodies."

"Strictly speaking you are right: gravitation is a screening effect. So I speak loosely. What the gun really did was to render Earth and the moon gravitationally transparent to one another.''

The *kosho* resumed his story. ''You will recall that after the fleet entered the region affected by the rent a number of persons vanished. Among them were myself, Pout and these two boys. We were instantaneously transported to the surface of a planet, the same, I think, that the fleet was headed for. I will not dwell on what took place there. Suffice to say that at last I procured the zen gun from Pout, and I was able to remedy the damage done by my fellow *kosho*. I used the gun to close up the rent.''

''So if you're telling the truth we don't have that to worry about anymore,'' Gruwert growled. ''Good.''

''You never did. The rent would have closed up by itself, after a while. Another problem was inadvertently solved, however. As the rent closed, the entities that had come through it withdrew. But first they restored everything to the condition in which they found it. Everything they had dismembered they put together, everything they had moved they put back, in the twinkling of an eye. Those of us from this ship were put back on this ship, mended in body if not in mind.''

''The fleet has moved light years since you were taken,'' Hesper said in puzzlement. ''If you were put back where you were before, it would be into the void.''

Ikematsu gave his faint smile. ''Evidently you have scant knowledge of physics. 'Place' as a physical reality applies only to material objects, not to empty space. This flagship is the 'place' from which we were taken, and it does not matter how it has altered its relationship with other places in the interim. Star Force's intermat system,'' he added casually, ''works on the same principle.''

''Then where is the zen gun now?'' Archier asked.

Ikematsu's head turned. He was looking to the door. Pout had suddenly appeared there. He walked with a tired slouch, head down, arms hanging, as the ape in him had taken over completely. Blinking, he stumbled into the room, swayed, then leaned against a wall.

With him was a boy of about eight who seemed to have been pushing Pout ahead of him. On seeing Gruwert, the boy saluted self-consciously. ''The chimera you ordered brought here, Admiral. We found him trying to hide in a clothes store. I, er, don't think he's very well.''

Feeling uneasy, Archier said, "That's all. Go now. At once."

As the boy left, Ikematsu answered Archier's question. "The gun was not on me when I reappeared aboard the flagship. I reason that it, too, must have returned to its point of departure. I surmise that Pout has it."

"*SMO Archier!*" Gruwert roared. "Get that gun!"

As if in a trance, Archier found himself moving towards the chimera, who suddenly flung up his arms to ward him off.

"No gun, no gun! Pout has no gun!"

"Look to see what you have in your bib, Pout," Ikematsu said gently.

Blankly Pout stared at him. Then, trembling, he dipped his hand in his garment. It came out holding the zen gun.

"No gun!" he screamed. "No gun!" In terror he flung it from him. It clattered to the floor.

Archier picked it up as it fell at his feet. He turned it over in his hand. It looked so ordinary, so unfinished. How much was he to believe of the *kosho*'s tale? It was extraordinary, but well within the bounds of possibility. What else could explain the behaviour of Earth's moon, for instance?

If the *kosho* really had woven this and other happenings into a concocted story, then he really was uncommonly inventive. Gruwert, at any rate, gave the tale credence. After only a brief glance at the weapon Archier was examining, he was calling for his bodyguard.

Ikematsu shook his head warningly. "Your stoat is asleep. I dealt with him earlier. You face me alone."

Gruwert shook with agitation. He knew how dangerous an adversary the *kosho* could be, even unarmed. He moved so as to put himself between Ikematsu and the door. "SMO," he ordered quickly, "get out of here fast and take that gun to safety. I'll hold this *kosho* back."

"No!" Hesper shrieked. "Don't let the pigs have it, or it's slavery forever!"

Archier froze, only vaguely aware that Hesper was moving towards him. His mind was filling with images. A vision of Axaline, the place where they were going. He knew full well what Gruwert intended. Nuke a city here, beam a continent there. And *then* demand tribute. The slightest resistance and . . .

Then, too, there was Escoria, Hesper's home sector. She claimed the fleet had nuked the moving teaching cities on

Earth. Archier no longer disbelieved it. It would be just like
Gruwert to arrange it behind his back.

And what a score he would settle with the sector as a
whole, when they next went there!

"Give *me* that gun!" It was Gruwert's voice, and it was
distorted with passion, with rage at Archier's lack of response.
Even as he spoke, the pig charged. He bowled Archier over,
reaching for the gun with his snout. Automatically Archier
tried to keep the gun from the animal's reach. The smell of
the pig was all over him. He felt bristly hide against his skin,
frantic trotters scrambling and trampling on his limbs and
body.

Then Hesper was with him, helping him struggle against
the bulging, vigorous mass of lard. Somehow she hauled him
from underneath Gruwert, who lost his balance and went
sprawling on his side.

Archier staggered to Ikematsu. He pressed the gun into his
hand. *"You* take it," he gasped. "Do whatever you can!"

Gruwert, snorting and squealing, trotters sliding on the
floor, raised himself. Furiously he turned to face the *kosho,*
backing off to charge him as he had Archier.

Before he could launch himself Ikematsu's hand swept up.
He spread two fingers, pointing them directly at the pig's two
eyes.

"Sleep."

And Gruwert stood there, as motionless as a statue, his
eyes open but unseeing.

As she joined Archier Hesper was breathing heavily. She
stared down at the pig. "What's wrong with him?" she
whispered.

"I have hypnotised him," Ikematsu said simply.

With a look of intent concentration on his face, he was
pressing the setting studs in a complicated sequence. "The
die is cast," he said to Archier. "You have made your
decision; you have committed treason against the pigs' Empire.
Now we must all leave."

"There's no way off this ship for us," Archier said, "unless
you know of one."

"Does not this gun reach into the Simplex? Have not the
scientists always assured us that access to the Simplex means
instantaneous travel to anywhere in our universe? Well, they
are right."

Again the *kosho*'s faint smile. He had finished what he was doing with the zen gun. He pointed the muzzle at each of his companions in turn, pressing the trigger stud each time.

The transition was without interval of time. Archier found himself standing on grassland in gathering dusk. The ground rose to a summit about a mile away, where he could see a building perched in outline against the darkening sky.

He was accustomed to using the intermat and so was not shocked or disoriented by the sudden change in surroundings, except that the air smelled unpleasantly bland and odourless. There were none of the additives he was used to, both on board ship and in the atmospheres of Diadem planets.

Then a breeze rippled the grass, and with it there came faint nameless scents.

He looked to see how Hesper had reacted. She seemed more bewildered than frightened, gazing about her with an expression of total bemusement. She had never used the intermat.

Pout had toppled over when deprived of the wall he had been leaning against and now sobbed with fear, until the *kosho* leaned over him and said something in a low, reassuring voice. He helped him to his feet.

"What planet is this?" Archier asked him.

"This is Earth."

"Earth?" echoed Hesper. "The planet we were on before? But that's impossible!"

"So everything you've told us about that gun is true." Archier nodded at the weapon which Ikematsu still held limply in his hand. The *kosho* nodded, putting it away somewhere in his robe.

Curiously, Archier looked at him. "Why didn't you help me when I was fighing with Gruwert?" he asked. "Why didn't you take the gun from the chimera yourself? You could have done that, probably. If it comes to that, why did you have to tell the pig about the gun at all?" He paused. "It's almost as if you set up what happened back there."

When Ikematsu didn't answer, Archier said, "I've heard *koshos* don't get involved in political causes. Is that true?"

"Anything you hear about *koshos* is liable to be untrue," Ikematsu said, with a hint of levity. Seriousness returned to his tone. "I will tell you the fact of it. My order has a rule: the *kosho* may not intervene directly in historical events. He may only act so as to create possibilities for actions by others. When I explained the nature of the zen gun to the pig, I was really speaking to you."

"And if I had stayed loyal to the Empire? Or if Gruwert had won? You wouldn't have interfered?"

"No."

Archier shook his head. "There's no point to this rule. It leaves everything to chance."

"The rule does not exist for the benefit of civilisation. It exists to preserve the *kosho* from corruption. Yet, paradoxically, because of it the order is better able to serve mankind. The zen gun was made because a *kosho* foresaw that the pigs would eventually seize power. He left it to chance to preserve his weapon until that time.

"This is why the gun's control is mental as well as manual. A pure animal cannot use it at all. The chimera Pout was able to use it a little, beause he is partly human. But he would never be able to unlock its real secrets. For that, a spiritually trained intelligence is needed."

"This *kosho* foresaw what the pigs would do? That long ago?" Archier was incredulous. "I can't believe it."

"But it was inevitable from the start. When you gave artifical intelligence to animals, you were giving base emotion an unnatural power of action. An animal with intelligence is still not equivalent to a man. It has no possibility of spiritual development, as a man has. This is easily proved. Animals do not experience what we call 'beauty,' for instance."

Archier frowned. It was true: they were beauty-blind, as the phrase had it. Implants didn't make any difference there.

"These creatures you have created should remain forever under the strict control of human beings," Ikematsu went on, the grimness of his words belied by the habitual matter-of-factness of his tone. "Base passions exist within man also, but his higher nature is able to contend with them. When animals became your equals in society, with the same power of thought and speech and action, that struggle was exteriorised. A minute or so ago, Admiral Archier, it depended upon you alone as to whether the future belonged to man or to the pig. And who is to say that the pig will not yet triumph? Have you the courage to become a warrior against his Empire? To use the zen gun against him?"

"I?"

Archier felt as if he had been struck a blow. "I am not a *kosho*."

"But you are a warrior." Ikematsu laughed, without humour. "A *kosho* will not use the gun in war, Admiral Archier. I just explained that. Neither does one need to be a *kosho* to use it. One needs a degree of mental training, that is all."

Lowering his head, Archier said, "What I just did is one thing, but I don't think I can bring myself to be traitor enough for what you are suggesting."

"Against the zen gun, the star fleets will be powerless to enforce obedience. But a man to use it must find the gun by himself. Well, we shall see. If my colleagues can analyse it successfully, the gun can be duplicated. Then the equaliser will remain always present . . ."

For a moment Ikematsu looked thoughtfully at Hesper. Then he pointed up the hill to the craggy outline. "That is a monastery where *koshos* receive part of their training. We shall go there now. The boy Trixa will be given mental therapy there."

He slapped Pout on the back. "This poor tormented creature, too, needs treatment. He should have a better education than life has given him so far. Come."

Slowly, moving as a group, they climbed through the slowly fading light to the looming, silent building.

Author's
Afterword

THE RECESSIVE HYPOTHESIS

The invented physics used in the background to this novel is very loosely based on a conjecture of my own of which I will give a cursory account. As I am not a scientist, and to my shame am not competent mathematically, it is unscientific and unquantified, but it has given me many hours of rewarding thought.

The conjecture arises from my conviction that gravitational attraction is impossible. My feelings about it can be illustrated as follows:

(1) Our experience of manipulating material objects is that we can move them about by pushing at them, i.e. applying force causes motion in the direction opposite to that from which the force came. Intuitively we feel this to be bound up with the form and character of the space in which we live, so that being able to draw an object towards us by means of magnetism or stickiness seems slightly mystifying.

(2) Randomly moving objects spread out with time, and this also is a feature of our spacetime. E.A. Milne gave the following as an example of irreversibility: a swarm of non-colliding particles movingly uniformly in straight lines will at some instant become an expanding system even if initially it was a contracting one. An already expanding system, however, will never become a contracting one.

Gravitation would be more explicable if it were repulsive instead of attractive. In physics the tendency is to regard forces of attraction and repulsion as opposite but otherwise equivalent, but the symmetry breaks down when the *milieu* in which they act is taken into account: the effect of repulsive forces weakens as they push their sources apart, but attractive force are able to act more strongly as they bring their sources together. The difference is crucial for world-building. Once again, it results from the 'form' of universal space, which permits limitless dispersal but not limitless convergence.

Its attractive character is only one of gravitation's mysterious properties, of course. Another is the equality between gravitational and inertial masses, which is the physicist's way of saying that all bodies fall with the same acceleration regardless of their masses. This equality makes it impossible to test Newton's third law of action and reaction with respect to gravitating bodies. Newton's expression for gravitational interaction between two bodies makes it a single force dependent on the products of the masses, and in this form it satisfies both gravitational and inertial equality and the third law, but this is a mathematical device. In reality it is to be supposed that each body exerts its own influence on the other, and a proper test of the third law would require the effects of each force taken separately to be measured.

What if gravitation *were* a force of repulsion? Since every piece of matter is surrounded by all the other matter in the whole universe, it is only necessary to suppose it is also opaque to the passage of the repulsive force for this force to be converted to one of apparent attraction between (relatively) close bodies. Earth and the moon are bound together because the pressure of the whole universe overcomes their native effort to separate. In one leap we have related gravitation to the recession of the galaxies.

The recessive hypothesis goes a step further. The equality of gravitational and inertial masses suggests that gravitation is not a force acting 'through' the immaterial 'something' we call space (as in the old ether theory) but is instead intimately implicated in the structure of space (as in general relativity). It is, therefore, a model of space that is called into play, one that answers to points (1) and (2) above.

The hypothesis posits primary locations which henceforth shall be called particles. The particles do not exist in isolation: they have a relationship with one another, and the relation is a dynamic one: they are all receding from one another at a standard uniform rate.

This recession is the major constituent of spacetime. It introduces, however, the rather abstruse concept of motion as an irreducible principle rather than a composite phenomenon played out against an already created backdrop of time and distance. Motion begins as the fundamental interaction, or mode of reciprocal existence, of the particles themselves. Time and distance are its emergent phenomena.

The idea can perhaps be conveyed with the remark that in receding from one another, the particles are not going towards anywhere else. This remains true of the receding galaxies.

Space, then, consists primarily of universal recession. In a sense the hypothesis revives the old principle of instantaneous action-at-a-distance, but this is because it pictures space as a dynamic connector of bodies, not as a static geometry.

In *The Zen Gun* there is talk of the Simplex, a state of existence in which recession is the only relation between particles. Our realm, however, could only accommodate a 4-simplex, or tetrahedron. In other words, it introduces geometrical relations as well as the recessive one. This means that a particle can interrupt the recessive link between other particles. When that happens, we shall assume the link is broken, and because of the law of perspective a pair of particles will each hide more of the celestial sphere from the other the closer together they are. What happens when a particle is receding from a greater number of particles in one direction than in another? Relativity has entered. We shall suppose the inequality to manifest itself in a lower overall rate of recession from the occluded region. Hence, the closer together bodies are in space, the slower is their rate of recession from one another.

If the distance between them is small enough, the recession is decremented sufficiently for them seemingly to attract one another. This is a definite transition. Their own mutual recession has become negative; for the first time particles are heading towards somewhere as they recede.

So apparently attractive forces are explained as an interference with a general arena of expansion. At the same time the degree in which a body's velocity is decremented (the acceleration it apparently acquires, if gravitating) is independent of its inertial mass. It is the velocities that have priority; inertial mass is stamped upon a particle by virtue of its recession from the surrounding universe. (This explanation is roughly similar to Mach's principle.)

As a by-product of decremented recession, we have to consider the recession lines connecting particles whose mutual recession has been slowed. These lines are still attempting to express their legitimate rate of expansion. There is something analogous to pressure upon them. A new class of effects is indicated, and to this we may assign electromagnetism.

An intriguing feature of magnetism is its similarity, in relation to electric force, with gyroscopic precession. In order to give an account of magnetism analogous to gyroscopic action, I concocted the notion of pseudospin described in Chapter 10. With a simple set of selection rules it becomes possible to give such an account, though the recession lines are treated as quasi-material. Also, the diagrams for electric attraction and repulsion become indistinguishable from already familiar lines of force.

The 'particles' spoken of so far are conceived of as a simpler form of neutron. The retarding of recession converts a part of its mass to positive charge so that it becomes a proton. This is followed by the creation of countervailing negative charge to make a neutron. The negative charge is then ejected to become an electron. Hydrogen is born.

The recessive hypothesis is so full of holes that it can be (and has been) dismissed as 'blind invention.' My strategy has been to get as much change out of it as possible, skirting difficulties and leaving them as unconquered fortresses in the rear, any one of them cogent enough to blow the conjecture's backside off. Just the same, it bears upon a sufficient number of additional questions, many of them previously unconnected, to make me think there might be a grain of truth in it. To mention a few:

1. Space is a continuum only along lines of recession. Across the grain, so to speak, it has discontinuous properties. Interesting from the point of view of the wave/particle dichotomy, and also because radiant energy consists of transverse waves.

2. A difficulty in the way of unifying the forces of nature has been that it is hard to imagine how one continuum could transmit them all. The recessive hypothesis offers a hierarchy of interpenetrating 'spaces' constructed of different sets of recession lines: (1) a space consisting of a single absolute velocity—the velocity of light—emanating from the matter at

the limit of the Hubble sphere; (2) a dynamic space of relative velocities and gravitation; (3) a subordinate space conveying electric force.

3. The hypothesis gives a physical basis to the idea of the inertial system. For argument's sake we can take an object's inertial framework to consist of the distant sphere of particles receding from it at the velocity of light. If it is accelerated to a new velocity then associated with that velocity will be a similar framework composed of a different set of particles (just as a galaxy anywhere finds itself at the centre of a symmetrically expanding system; the object, however, will be displaced from the centre of its system)—so it continues in its state of motion. Without recession, dynamics might be what Aristotle thought it was: applying a force produces not acceleration but a uniform motion, which stops when the force stops.

4. It is possible to save the perfect cosmological principle, which requires that the distribution of the galaxies should be roughly the same at any epoch. The primary recession is an interaction antecedent to time or spatial distance. It is therefore conceivable that the equation between time and distance is not applicable at very long range. The farther galaxies could be receding from us *without getting any farther away*.

5. It is an appealing idea that recession leads both to gravitation and to the universal property of dispersal we know as the second law of thermodynamics. It would mean that water falling through a water turbine is answering to the same principle as steam expanding through a steam turbine.

6. Attributing the two forms of electric force to the two directions of pseudospin explains the breakdown of parity in some experiments. The mirror image of a negative charge is a positive charge. Parity is conserved if the signs are switched.

7. Finally, the recessive hypothesis is the answer to the paradoxes of Zeno on the impossibility of motion. I will not repeat them here (for an illuminating discussion of them, see G.J. Whitrow's *The Natural Philosophy of Time*) but the three relevant paradoxes 'prove' that (1) a fast runner cannot overtake a slow one, (2) an arrow cannot reach its target, and (3) the arrow can't move at all anyway.

From the point of view of the recessive hypothesis, Zeno's paradoxes aren't paradoxes at all. They are demonstrations that what we see as motion is impossible. Therefore it must be something else.

What the arguments do is to destroy the concept of *place:* the idea that a physical object occupies a location in a receptive space and can move 'through space' to another such location. In the recessive hypothesis space is purely relational; there is no 'place' except where a physical body is. When such a body appears to 'move' in relation to another, it is the space between them that is modified. The objects stay in the same 'place,' i.e., they simply remain themselves.

The same insight is admirably expressed in the zen aphorism: 'Nothing moves; where would it go?'

A GALAXY OF SCIENCE FICTION STARS!